CATAWAMPUS Christmas CAROL

DEADWOOD UNDERTAKER SERIES
Book 3.5

Ann Charles
Sam Lucky

2020 Ann Charles & Sam Lucky

This one is dedicated to our children, Beaker and Chicken Noodle. Over the years, you've experienced many Christmas adventures with us far from home without a single complaint. We love you!
(Now let's pack up and experience the holiday festivities somewhere new.)

Catawampus Christmas Carol

Copyright © 2020 by Ann Charles and Sam Lucky

All rights reserved. Except as permitted under the U.S. Copyright Act of 1976, no part of this publication may be reproduced, distributed, or transmitted in any form or by any means now known or hereafter invented, or stored in a database or retrieval system, without the prior written permission of the author, Ann Charles.

This book is a work of fiction. Names, characters, places, and incidents are the product of the author's imagination or are used fictitiously. Any resemblance to actual persons, living or dead, business establishments, events, or locales is coincidental.

Cover Design by AC & BB
Editing by Eilis Flynn
Formatting by B Biddles

Library of Congress Control Number: 2020923810
E-book ISBN- 978-1-940364-76-6
Print ISBN-: 978-1-940364-77-3

Dear Reader

We are big fans of the movie *Scrooged* with Bill Murray. So, when it came time to plan a Christmas novella for the Deadwood Undertaker crew, following along the lines of *Scrooged* (which in turn follows along the lines of Dickens' *A Christmas Carol*) felt like the right path to travel. So, if you know the movie/story—either one or both—we hope you'll enjoy finding and exploring the parallels throughout our novella, *Catawampus Christmas Carol*. Without further ado, we bid you a merry Christmas and a happy New Year! May your life be blessed with laughter and friendship and lots of books!

Sam and Ann

Acknowledgments

Many thanks to all who have helped make this novella sparkle and shine!

Eilis Flynn (our editor); our first draft crew for this story—Margo Taylor, Mary Ida Kunkle, Wendy Gildersleeve, Kristy McCaffrey, Vicki Husky, Lucinda Nelson, Michelle Davis, and Diane Garland; our kickbutt beta crew; and Bill Murray for his wonderful portrayal of Frank Cross (aka Scrooge).

Also by Ann Charles

Deadwood Undertaker Series
(written with Sam Lucky)
Life at the Coffin Joint (1)
A Long Way from Ordinary (2)
Can't Ride Around It (3)
Catawampus Christmas Carol (3.5)
The Backside of Hades (4) (in 2021)

Jackrabbit Junction Mystery Series
Dance of the Winnebagos (1)
Jackrabbit Junction Jitters (2)
The Great Jackalope Stampede (3)
The Rowdy Coyote Rumble (4)
The Wild Turkey Tango (4.5)
In Cahoots with the Prickly Pear Posse (5)

Deadwood Mystery Series

Nearly Departed in Deadwood (1)
Optical Delusions in Deadwood (2)
Dead Case in Deadwood (3)
Better Off Dead in Deadwood (4)
An Ex to Grind in Deadwood (5)
Meanwhile, Back in Deadwood (6)
Wild Fright in Deadwood (7)
Rattling the Heat in Deadwood (8))
Gone Haunting in Deadwood (9)
Don't Let It Snow in Deadwood (10)
Devil Days in Deadwood (11)

Deadwood Shorts: Seeing Trouble (Book 1.5)
Deadwood Shorts: Boot Points (Book 4.5)
Deadwood Shorts: Cold Flame (Book 6.5)
Deadwood Shorts: Tequila & Time (Book 8.5)
Deadwood Shorts: Fatal Traditions (Book 10.5)

Dig Site Mystery Series
Look What the Wind Blew In (Book 1)
Make No Bones About It (Book 2)

AC Silly Circus Mystery Series
Feral-LY Funny Freakshow (Novella 1)
A Bunch of Monkey Malarkey (Novella 2)

Goldwash Mystery Series (a future series)
The Old Man's Back in Town (Short Story)

STAVE ONE

Uncle Mort's Ghost

Once upon a time ...

Actually, it was Christmas Eve 1876 in the rough and tumble mining town of Deadwood (Dakota Territory), but anyway ...

"Uncle Mort is dead," Jack "Rabbit" Fields told his longtime friend and partner in the livery and soon-to-be hotel business.

"There's no doubt whatsoever about that," Boone McCreery replied, leaning against a freight wagon loaded with rough-cut planks that were destined to become part of The Sidewinder Hotel the two of them were in the process of building. He aimed a wrinkled brow at Rabbit. "I was standing next to you at Uncle Morton's funeral, remember? Or has that McCuddle's Original Magical Tonic you love to snuggle with through the night muddled your mind?"

Rabbit scooped up a handful of snow, packed it, and threw it at the wiseacre. "Of course I remember, lunkhead. My point being, now that Uncle Mort's no longer breathing, it's up to you and me to continue with his favorite holiday traditions, including takin' the day off to prepare for the big celebrations happenin' tomorrow."

Still frowning, Boone wiped the snow off his coat. "This lumber isn't going to unload itself, Rabbit." He rounded the end of the wagon loaded with stacked planks.

"Booney, you're beginnin' to remind me of Ebenezer Scrooge, insisting I work in the freezin' cold on Christmas Eve. I'm feelin' like Scrooge's assistant, poor Mr. Cratchit."

"Cratchit was Scrooge's clerk, not his assistant." Boone grabbed the end of a plank. "Your tail is dragging because you can't figure out what I got you for Christmas. Now pick up the other end of this plank and let's get on with your next guess. You only get eight more, you know."

Of course Rabbit knew. They'd only played this game since they were kids sharing a room on Uncle Mort's ranch down in Santa Fe. "I can eat it," he said, confident in his answer, and then he hefted the end of the twenty-foot piece of lumber.

His friendship with Boone had sprouted and grown since they were tykes some quarter century ago. That being an age-old fact, it wasn't difficult for Rabbit to read the glow of evil delight on Boone's face in spite of the dark beard shadowing everything south of his nose. Rabbit's guess about being able to eat it must have been miles from close.

"Nooo. You can't eat it." Boone chuckled after they dropped the plank on top of the others next to the hotel's foundation.

So it wasn't vittles. Rabbit returned to the wagon and lifted the end of another plank. "You gonna show me your muscles, you big strong man?" He nodded once at the plank. "Pick that end up."

"Give up?" Boone grunted as he hefted his end up to his chest. Without a word, they heaved in unison and lay the plank on the growing stack.

Rabbit wasn't about to quit guessing at what his *compadre* was giving him for Christmas. "Does it snow on a camel in the woods?"

Boone did a double-take. "What does that mean?"

"It means I don't give up. Is it big?"

"Depends."

"How can somethin' like that *depend*?" Rabbit clapped his half-frozen hands together to keep the blood from freezing in his fingers, then grabbed another plank and with Boone's help slid it out of the wagon.

They'd started early, before the sun had made a proper entrance and the gusts roiling up the streets of Deadwood still had the bitter bite of night in them. For the last hour, Rabbit had worked at keeping the cold bug from stinging his ass and giving him a case of depression. His thick sheepskin coat and canvas trousers weren't much of a match for a Black Hills winter night, not even when he dressed in layers with an extra pair of long underwear beneath it all.

"Hold on." Boone pulled his gloves off, tucked them into the crook of his arm, and blew into his hands. He wore pretty much the same garb as Rabbit, only his gloves were newer, his wool hat was thicker, and he was wearing *two* extra pair of socks.

Rabbit crossed his arms. "I remember some old tinhorn who's always offering advice—unwelcome advice, mind you—tellin' me that blowin' in my hands only makes them colder."

"That was me." Boone rubbed his hands together, grinning under his frosty moustache.

"Yep. Sounds like you."

"I'm six months older than you, so I'm not *old*. And tinhorn?" Boone scoffed. "I may be truculent at times, but a tinhorn?" He slipped his hands back into his gloves while shaking his head.

Rabbit bobbled his head. "*I may be truculent*," he repeated in a deeper voice, imitating Boone. The old tinhorn didn't even realize when he was being a windbag.

"Shut up, donkey." Boone pointed at the next plank. "Lift."

Rabbit shoved the plank toward Boone and started to lift the end just as a dog yelped and then howled down the street. He stilled, his mind returning to the damp darkness of the Bloody Bones mine in a blink. A sea of howling, snarling beasties flooded his thoughts. Slick dark fur, massive shoulders, dagger-like teeth and claws. The pack of *Bahkauv* swarmed around him.

He shuddered and dropped the end of the plank. Sweat formed on his brow in spite of the frigid gusts that wheedled in through his coat. The vicious creatures haunted his memories and cast shadows on the cold reality that had been solid and bright a moment before.

"Rabbit?" Boone's face emerged through the vision of swarming *Bahkauv*. He grasped Rabbit by the shoulders. "You feeling fit, *Cochito*? Steady now."

His heart hammering, he focused on Boone's face. *Cochito?* He must be in worse shape than he thought. Boone used that name only when they were alone and things were serious.

His legs wobbly all of a sudden, Rabbit leaned into Boone's steady grip.

"Easy, *amigo*." Boone's voice was low and soothing.

The sinister, growling beasties retreated back into the dark corners of Rabbit's mind.

"Wh … what was that?" Rabbit wiped his sleeve across his brow and straightened, his legs steady once again.

Boone loosened his hold but didn't let go. "Tell me."

"*Bahkauv*."

Boone nodded, his dark eyes full of understanding for all that came with that single word.

"You think we got 'em all, Booney?"

He let go of Rabbit and blew out his cheeks. "I'd be a kitten with a bowl of cream if I could say *yes*."

"Yeah. The recollection of those beasties does me in a little every single time it hits."

Boone studied him. "Back to the load?"

A wiggle of movement behind his *compadre* caught Rabbit's attention. Rabbit squinted in the dim, early light. "Uncle Mort!" His dead uncle's ghost stood next to a wagon that looked quite a bit like the fancy Mitchell the old codger used to drive when pulling freight. "What are you doin' over there? Why are you waving at me?"

And what was that on his head?

He frowned as Uncle Mort float-walked toward him, his long threadbare, light blue winter nightgown undulating with a current that had nothing to do with the stiff breezes blowing through the gulch. As he drew closer, Uncle Mort's form became clearer, less fuzzy around the edges. On his head sat the knitted, tasseled nightcap he wore on cold evenings back in Santa Fe; on his feet were a pair of old boots—the ones he wore to do rounds at the ranch before settling in for the night.

"You keep throwing conniptions when I come up from behind." He shook his palms at Rabbit. "Don't want to compromise your healthy mindedness. You skirt dangerous close to 'gone over' as it is."

"I'm dangerous close to 'gone over' because of you, that much you got right." Standing here talking to his dead uncle in broad daylight would likely send Rabbit into a lunatic asylum before he … "Wait a goldurn minute! I'm not close to 'gone over,' you ol' coot."

"That may or may not be true," Boone interrupted. "I guess Uncle Morton decided to present himself this morning? To *you*, anyway. Tell him we could use a hand unloading."

"Someday, Booney, you'll see him, too." So far, Uncle Mort's ghost seemed to be visible only to Rabbit. Although Tinker, his uncle's three-legged dog, seemed mighty disturbed whenever Uncle Mort's ghost hovered near her. "And you know good and well Uncle Mort can hear you."

"Surely." Boone shook his head, though.

"His mind isn't open to it," Uncle Mort said, combing the fringe on the tassel of his nightcap. "Tell him I'd like to converse with him."

Tell him … Rabbit huffed. "Well, you're stuck with me, Uncle Mort." He pointed at his still-living *compadre*. "This is your fault, Booney. Too many books! Me? I'm open to possibilities. But your way of thinkin' is all overfilled with big words."

"Is that right?" Boone folded his arms.

"Yep. Uncle Mort says you're not open to it."

"Is that all? Open up, he says?" Boone's moustache twitched.

"Yep. He says you need a dressin' down."

Uncle Mort's ghostly pale forehead furrowed. "That's not what I said."

"That's what I heard," Rabbit shot back at his uncle. "I got it wrong? You go on ahead and tell him yourself." He picked up his end of a plank. "Let's get this done, Booney."

Uncle Mort stood by and watched Boone and Rabbit as they finished unloading the wagon.

Rabbit kept an eye on his uncle as he worked while a mixture of irritation and uncertainty and gratefulness clouded his thoughts.

Why was he the only one who could see and talk to his uncle's ghost?

Uncle Mort had previously told Rabbit that he'd considered his job of raising Rabbit to manhood to be incomplete, unlike Boone, whom he'd called a "fine man." So, Uncle Mort had returned in his current wispy form to finish the job. But why wasn't Rabbit "man" enough yet?

And why was his uncle so much more irascible since his death? Had the escape from his flesh freed this contrary attitude, or was he suffering from a case of frustration for the way things used to be?

Rabbit glanced over and caught Boone eyeing him with worry lines on his face. "I'm fine, I'm tellin' ya."

Boone nodded. "That was a spell is all?"

"Yeah. I think when that dog got to howlin' down the street, that set me off."

"I'm not surprised. Thoughts like that wake me some nights."

"Same here." Rabbit looked up and down the street. "Where are Ling and Gart with that other wagon? We need to get that unloaded, too." The two gravediggers were moonlighting as carpenters and freighters these days since the frozen ground interfered with burying bodies.

"I'll head up, assess the delay." Boone closed the wagon's gate and started toward the street.

"You're walkin'?" Rabbit called after him.

"Take longer to saddle Nickel than it will to walk. Few minutes and I'll be at the lumber mill." Boone waved and headed off.

"*Bahkauv.*" Uncle Mort shimmered into a wavy mess. "Foul creatures."

"We took care of 'em, Uncle Mort. Horses did their share, too. They took down ten or fifteen. That black beauty of Clementine's did most of that. Dime did a lot of runnin'. Ol' Fred the Mule skedaddled, though." Rabbit started straightening the stack of planks.

"Clementine? You mean that handsome Amazon in the livery?" Uncle Mort pushed at the planks to help with straightening them, but his hands went right through the lumber.

Rabbit stretched his back from side to side, working out the kinks as he thought about Clementine Johanssen. Uncle Mort's description of her as an Amazon was fitting. She was extra long-legged for a woman and strong enough to toss a blacksmith's anvil clear across the Rio Grande. On top of those jaw-dropping virtues, the woman had a streak of stubborn independence that was out-matched only by the fierceness of her character.

It was that same fierceness that kept *almost* getting her into trouble. And by trouble, Rabbit meant the heart-stopping sort at the hands of beasties and other unfriendly non-human folks. Not that Clementine wasn't accustomed to strong-arming such troublemakers, but since coming to Deadwood, her carefully scripted routine of solitary existence had been disrupted—first by Hank, her unabashedly loyal associate … no, make that friend; and then by Boone and Rabbit, fresh up from Santa … *Hold up!*

"What?" Rabbit squinted at his uncle. "She's in the livery?"

"This very moment." Uncle Mort gave up on helping

straighten the lumber and sat on the stack instead. Well, more like hovered above it. "She's saddling that big black 'Beauty,' as you call her. That surely is a grand animal. Some rascal whipped that horse, though. Got the scars to prove it."

"She said she had notes to take today," Rabbit said to himself more than his uncle. "Told us she'd see us tomorrow. For Christmas." It would be like Clementine to … He kicked at a lump of snow, sending slush flying right through his uncle. "Jehoshaphat!"

"Now what'd you do that for?" Uncle Mort snorted. "That darn temper of yours is going to be your undoing, boy."

Ignoring his uncle, Rabbit sprinted the few steps to the livery and flung open the door. "Miss Clementine!" He paused inside the door while his eyes adjusted to the darkness. The smell of horseflesh, straw dust, and blacksmithing coal greeted him as he stepped farther into the barn's interior. "Miss Clementine! You in here?"

"*Verdammt!*" he heard her curse.

Rabbit squinted at the shadows in the direction of Clementine's voice. As his eyes adjusted, he could see that she had saddled and geared up Fenrir, her majestic black Morgan, and was preparing to lead the horse out of the livery. As for Clementine herself, the flaps on her fur-lined hat were down, covering her ears. Her long auburn braid looked like a tail trailing down from the back of the hat. She had a red knitted scarf wrapped around her neck, gloves tucked halfway into the pockets of her wool coat, and canvas trousers crammed into tall boots that reached her knees.

"Mornin'." He sauntered up next to her and made a point of taking in the gear on Fenrir's back. Bedroll. Haversack stuffed with who knew what. Saddlebags bulging with … blades? "That might be considered more than a fair amount of sharp steel in there."

Clementine sighed. "I thought you and Boone were busy

working on the hotel."

She must have seen them unloading the planks on her way into the livery. "Now, if Boone was standin' here, I do believe he'd call that a look of dismay." Rabbit slowly circled Clementine and Fenrir, careful to stay a fair distance from the end of the horse that had teeth. "As in, 'Her escape nearly realized, Miss Clementine's hopes were sunk and she was overcome with *dismay* at the sight of Mr. Jack Fields. You see, with his exceedingly ample intellect, Mr. Fields reckoned she was contemplating heading toward the backside of Hell.' And by *Hell*, I'm referrin' to ... oh, I don't know, maybe Slagton?"

Her lips curled slightly at the corners. "I'm not sure that I'd say 'overcome' with dismay."

Amelia Beaman, the daughter of the blacksmith Rabbit and Boone had recently hired, appeared from the shadows carrying a bucket heavy with grain in one hand and dragging a metal chain in her other. "Good morning, Miss Johanssen, Mr. Fields." Happiness rang in her voice this morning.

Like Clementine, Amelia was wearing trousers. However, their new horse wrangler was petite and slender where Clementine was taller than most men and built to pull a plow through mud. Although, judging by the full bucket Amelia was hauling without much effort, she was plenty strong as well under her men's clothing. What was she planning to do with that chain?

"Good morning, Amelia." Clementine smiled at the girl.

Rabbit nodded in greeting, clearing his throat before adding, "Happy Christmas Eve, Amelia."

His stomach fluttered when she stared back at him. With her cheeks turning bright pink from exertion and her dark hair swirling around her pretty face, Rabbit was having trouble looking away this morning. How old had Hank figured the girl was? Early twenties?

"I should have saddled Fenrir for you, Miss Johannsen." Amelia stopped next to Clementine and lowered the bucket so she could stroke down along Fenrir's neck and shoulder. Then she took up her bucket and chain and moved along.

"I didn't want to bother you. Thought you might still be asleep." Clementine waited while Amelia crossed the livery to a pair of horses nodding and nickering at the sight of the grain bucket before turning her attention back to Rabbit. "I'll be gone just one day," she said for his ears only. "Back tomorrow for Christmas supper most likely."

Rabbit made a show of pursing his lips and shaking his head slowly, as if he were disappointed in Clementine's sneaking off like this. He wasn't, really. It didn't surprise him at all, her being prepared to light out alone. Clementine had been a lone wolf for a long time. She'd been trained by her grandfather when she was a youngster how to hunt all by herself and rely only on her own strengths.

"Listen, Jack." She kept her voice low. "You and Boone are busy with the hotel and this place." She thumbed toward the rest of the livery. "I can handle Slagton. Besides, I just want to take a look around out there, that's all."

Rabbit tipped his head, his lips still pressed together.

"Don't look at me like that." Clementine fidgeted with the gear on Fenrir's back. "I don't need company everywhere I go." She glanced at Rabbit. "I'm a grown woman."

Rabbit crossed his arms. "I'm not inclined to argue that point," he said. "But I'm not inclined to let you ride off alone to a mining town full of ambulators plucked from the ground, neither. Boone would tan my hide if I let you do that. And Hank would fret away all the hair on his head."

Clementine's eyes widened. She looked pointedly at Amelia, who was dumping the bucket of grain in a trough at the far end of the livery. She stepped closer to Rabbit. "There's no need to be spreading talk of …" She trailed off, glancing toward Beaman's daughter again, and then leaned toward him and continued in a hushed voice, "Of the ambulating recently deceased."

Rabbit waved her off. "Amelia's way over there." Although the busy *señorita* was making her way back toward them now, still dragging that darn chain.

"And no one said Slagton is 'full' of *Draug*," Clementine whispered in spite of Amelia's distance from them. "For all we know, there might only be a handful corralled out there." She patted Fenrir's side. "I'm determined to find out for sure, though, sooner rather than later."

"Right. Well, if you're set on goin', I need to get Dime tacked up." He frowned toward the livery door. "I'd just as soon we wait for Hank and Boone, but that's your decision."

"I'll get Dime for you, Mr. Fields," Amelia called. She headed toward the stall shared by Nickel and Dime, Boone and Rabbit's horses.

He frowned at Amelia. "She hears good," he said under his breath.

The hard-headed woman next to him grunted. "I told you. She listens." When Rabbit turned back to Clementine, he ran smack-dab into her scowling expression. "There's no need to get Dime, Amelia," she said loud and clear. "Mr. Fields isn't going anywhere. He's working on his hotel today." She stepped closer, adding quietly, "And he's not going to say a word about this to anyone. Right, Mr. Fields?"

He returned her stare with a defiant glare. Hank's mule, Fred, had nothing on Clementine when it came to stubbornness. "Saddle Dime up, Amelia. I'll go get my pack." And his knives and guns, too. Uncle Mort hadn't raised Rabbit to be a spineless milksop. If she was going to go riding into Slagton, then he was going to be there to stab and stick anything that needed to be stabbed and stuck.

"Mr. Fields?" Amelia stood next to Dime's stall, worrying her lower lip.

"It's 'Jack,' Amelia. Call me Jack. Or Rabbit."

She draped the chain over the stall door. "Mr. Jack, after I saddle Dime, would you or Mr. McCreery mind terrible if I decorate some today? Here in the livery, I mean? For Christmas?"

Christmas.

A flurry of warm thoughts rushed through him. All of those happy holiday times on their ranch in Santa Fe with Lupe, the ranch's cook, filling trays with mouth-watering, fried *buñuelos* sprinkled with shaved sugar; Carlos, their foreman, setting out paper lanterns, crafting colorful tin ornaments to hang in the windows, and painting gourds for the dinner table's centerpiece; Boone lugging branches of juniper and piñon pine inside to decorate the mantel and sills; Uncle Mort ...

The flood of memories slowed, his mind focusing on Uncle Mort's smiling face, silver whiskers, and ruddy cheeks.

Rabbit's heart sank down to his belly. With Uncle Mort gone, this would be the first Christmas without the old codger since Rabbit and Boone's parents perished on the wagon trip out West when the boys were just knee-high to those big grasshoppers that swarmed the plains.

"Someone say *Christmas*?" Uncle Mort appeared *through* the livery door, as if Rabbit had conjured him for real—well, as real as a ghost could be. "I do loooove *Navidad* and all its trimmings." He chortled in his close-yet-far-away ghostly echo.

Rabbit watched his uncle swoop through the air with happiness. Make that the first Christmas without Uncle Mort for Boone, anyway.

"Lupe's *arroz con leche,*" Uncle Mort sang out, now twirling in circles around the livery, as if dancing with a most beloved partner. "*Tamales.* Creamy *coquito.* Crunchy *tostones.* Mmm."

Uncle Mort had always done Christmas in the biggest way he could. Lots of presents and lots of food. It was a weeklong *fiesta* for Uncle Mort, and he insisted that his "nephews" share in all of the festivities, too. Throughout that week, his uncle carried on a love affair with the pageantry and the spectacle of what he considered a proper Christmas celebration. From the ribbons and yarn that decorated his dog Tinker's house to the grandest evergreen tree, cut from the foothills of the Sangre de Cristo Mountains near Santa Fe. Candles everywhere, stockings stuffed full of ...

"Lupe's *cochitos*!" Uncle Mort twirled to a stop beside Rabbit. "You have molasses. You must! To make *cochitos* you must have molasses!" His ear-to-ear grin pushed his cheeks clear up to his eyes. "*Cochitos.* Little pigs. You remember?" Uncle Mort smiled down at Rabbit. "Boone called you *Cochito*—the little piggy that ate all the little piggies!" Uncle Mort began twirling again, his deep belly laugh rumbling up to the rafters. "Ha ha! Wonderful! We must make them." He swooped back toward Rabbit, swaying gently in front of him as if drifting in a small pool. "Does Boone still call you *Cochito*?"

He didn't wait for Rabbit's confirmation, taking up an imaginary partner again and waltzing across the livery toward Tinker, who was now short of one hind leg thanks to those damned *Bahkauv*. The little dog spun in circles of her own, apparently sensing the excitement floating around her since she didn't seem to be able to see Uncle Mort's ghost. She barked twice at the air and then raced from one end of the livery to the other, her missing leg not slowing her down a bit.

A hint of a smile crept onto Rabbit's face as he watched his uncle dance and Tink run and yip and play. He couldn't help it. Uncle Mort's delight was contagious. It always had been. Even Tink felt it.

"You two boys always had such fun on Christmas," Uncle Mort said. He leaned down to catch Tink on her way back toward him, but the dog raced right through his long nightgown, which made Uncle Mort let out another drumroll of belly laughs.

"Jack?" Clementine rested her hand on Rabbit's shoulder.

He snorted in surprise at her touch. "Uh, yeah. Okay." He

scratched his chin. "What?"

"I asked if you're feeling okay." Clementine took up Fenrir's lead line.

Amelia led Dime past them into the tack stall. "I'll have him ready in the shake of a lamb's tail, Mr. Fields ... I mean, Mr. Jack." As usual, Dime nickered to Amelia continuously as she worked on him. Rabbit had never known his horse to talk so much, not even to Nickel. Not until meeting Amelia.

"Don't bother. Jack is staying here." Clementine led Fenrir to the door of the livery. "Tell Boone and Hank not to come after me. I'll be fine." She stepped out into the early morning pale light.

"Goldurnit, Miss Clementine!" Rabbit ran after her. He caught up to her in time to see her glance down Deadwood's main street and then freeze in her tracks. "Odin's beard!" she cursed and shook her fist at the sky.

Rabbit followed her line of sight—Hank was walking their way, leading Fred the Mule along behind him.

"Mornin', Miss Clem!" Hank called, slowing to a stop in front of her. "Caught you at the start of it, did I?" Hank checked her out from top to bottom and then shot a quick look at Fenrir's load. "Looks like the makin's of an adventure."

If anyone knew what an adventure looked like, it was Hank Varney. The man claimed to be a few years north of forty, but something about the gravel in his voice, the whip-cord leanness of his form, the weathered lines on his face, and the grit in his never-ending gumption gave the feeling of a soul much, much older, not to mention thickly calloused by life. Yet whenever Hank came around, he spread cheer without even trying.

Clementine's shoulders drooped under the weight of Hank's scrutiny. "So it would seem." She knew, as well as Rabbit, that Hank could be a formidable force when he set his mind to a task, and it was clear to see by the older man's downturned mouth that he wasn't kicking up his heels at Clementine heading off without him.

Rabbit grinned, his spirits lifted in part because of his uncle's festive carrying-on inside the livery, but more so now thanks to the arrival of reinforcements. Any trepidation he'd felt about letting Clementine venture forth into the wilds of Slagton solo would be undoubtedly doubled by Hank's feelings on the matter.

The older man would do his darnedest to drag anchor when it came to her venturing off without them, Rabbit had no doubt. If that weren't enough, Rabbit was happy to try his hand at peddling the pleasure of celebrating the holiday here amongst her friends instead of out there in bad company. And he was most certain Boone would join their ranks soon as he heard tell of Clementine's solitary plans. Between the three of them, her notion to go gallivanting off on Christmas Eve would be done for.

"Good timing, Hank." Rabbit rubbed his gloved hands together. "If I didn't know better, I'd say a certain hard-headed ol' ghost paid you a visit and sent you this way to see Miss Clementine before she headed off to Slagton."

"Slagton, ya say?" Hank hung his head low, the sorrowful look in his eyes no doubt aimed right at Clementine's soft spot. "Oh, now, Miss Clem. I thought we was waitin' 'til after Christmas for that business."

Clementine regarded him for a moment, her expression stony, but then her focus shifted and she began a deliberate inspection of Hank's mule. "Is Christmas really worth the effort, Hank?"

She patted an overly stuffed canvas bag strapped to Fred the Mule's side. A matching sack hung heavy over the other side. On top, a crate big enough to make a man grunt and wheeze while lifting it sat perched and roped on his croup. Smaller muslin and cotton sacks tied shut with twine and wire hung in disarray around the larger items.

Rabbit's gaze dropped to the forlorn-looking mule shifting from hoof to hoof under the bulging load. "Poor ol' Fred. Like to break his back with all this consignment, Hank."

Hank patted Fred's shoulder. His brow knitted as he looked the mule in the eye. "Penance, ain't it, boy? Penance for skedaddlin' on a pard." Hank waved toward Rabbit. "Two pards. Left us standin' outside that mine with our pants down." He glanced downward quickly, his cheeks darkening. "Sorry, Miss Clem. But ol' Fred left us standin' at the Bloody Bones. All them *Bahkauv*." Hank shook his finger at Fred. "Left Nickel. Left Dime. Even Fenrir here. Left us all, didn't ya?"

Fred's head drooped so low his nose nearly touched the snow. Rabbit would have laughed if the mule didn't look so darned forlorn.

Fenrir snorted and pawed at the broken ice beneath her feet, interrupting Hank's lecture. When it came to hitting the trail, the black beauty usually suffered from a terrible itch to get a mosey on. But this time, Fenrir sidled over as close as she could to the cargo-laden mule and nuzzled him, nickering softly.

"Whad'ya know about that?" Hank tipped his sweat-stained hat and rubbed his forehead. "Never seen her do such a thing."

"Fenrir's got herself a smidgeon of compassion under that cob-rough demeanor." Rabbit winked at Clementine. "Reminds me of somebody."

Clementine raised her brow, feigning ignorance, but there was a slight curve to her lips. "Why, who might you mean, Jack?" She turned to Hank, her smile spreading further up her cheeks. "Fenrir is a good judge of character."

Hank nodded once. "She is at that."

"Fred the Mule is loyal and durable," she continued. "While he may not be in for the battle, he gets all of us where we need to be every time. He knows the way. He reminds me of Sleipnir, Odin's eight-legged horse in Norse mythology. Sleipnir was described as the 'best of all horses,' and Odin sometimes even rode him into Hel, the Norse underworld." She paused and scratched behind Fred's ears. "Only Fred's a mule and he's not gray with eight legs, but you get my point."

"He surely cuts the trail for us," Rabbit agreed. "You do too, Hank. Two bugs in a bed, you boys are."

Hank rubbed the back of his neck. "Suppose you both are right. Fred does his part. Just got to know what to expect from a body is all."

"Right." Clementine eyed the load burdening Fred. "Now, what is all this?"

"Delivering supplies?" Rabbit wondered.

Hank tightened a rope that was beginning to sag. "That about sums it, Jack Rabbit."

"You loaded that all by yourself, Hank?" Clementine asked and then sprang onto Fenrir's back, settling in for the ride to Slagton.

"Miss Clementine, don't go off now." Rabbit looked back at the livery's open door, trying to peer inside. He couldn't see anything but shadows, darn it. "Amelia's almost got Dime saddled," he fibbed.

"Miss Clem, you done brought me to my conundrum." Hank grabbed Fenrir's lead line and looked up at Clementine with big puppy-dog eyes. "If'n you'd just come down for a spell, I'll explain it to you."

"What is it?" She didn't budge from her saddle.

"Now I know you want to get on the trail. But I wonder if'n you might lend me a helpin' hand. Just take a minute or three. Maybe a li'l longer. Then you can be off."

Rabbit frowned. Hank was being uncharacteristically agreeable to the idea of Clementine riding into the hellhole of a mining camp very possibly filled with more than a handful of deadly troublemakers. Alone.

"Jack and Boone are here to lend you a hand, Hank," she replied offhandedly, her gaze aimed up the street.

"No can do, Miss Clementine," Rabbit said, finally catching on to Hank's game. "I got a freighter to unload soon as Boone gets back with Ling and Gart."

"I'll be needin' *your* help, Miss Clem." Hank emphasized his insistence by pointing his finger at her. "You know it's not often I ask for much from ya." Knowing Hank, Rabbit figured he took no pleasure in manipulating Clementine, but desperate times called for whatever it took to stop the obstinate woman from charging Hell on her own.

Clementine looked at the sky and shook her head. "Great hall of Valhalla!" she muttered. In a blink, she slid from Fenrir's back and stood before Hank again, arms folded, chin jutted. "Needing my help with what, Hank?"

Hank handed Fenrir's lead line to Rabbit, sending him a quick wink on the sly. Then he turned and led Fred the Mule down the street toward Chinatown. "This way, Miss Clem. Fred will cut the trail, just like Jack Rabbit said."

Grumbling under her breath, Clementine took off after him.

"Miss Clem, I ever tell you about the Christmas I spent in New Orleans?" Rabbit heard Hank say as they moseyed off.

While Fenrir snorted steam and pawed at the snow, Rabbit watched as the three of them—man, woman, and mule—merged into the growing commotion of a busy little mining town on the day before Christmas.

STAVE TWO

The First
of the Three Friends

Clementine had guessed the jig to which Mr. Hank Varney danced after one stop; and she'd confirmed her conclusion after they halted thrice more. A half-dozen more adjourns since leaving Jack and the livery behind, and she'd given up on trying to hurry Hank along completely.

Every time he'd paused their procession, Hank would unstring a bag or box or both and carry it into a saloon, or shack, or tent while Clementine waited in the frigid morning gusts with Fred the Mule. She'd even taken to hugging Fred's neck to share body heat ... at least that was the story she was sticking to if caught with her arms around the ornery beast of burden.

After a short time—and sometimes not so short—Hank would return carrying a different bag or box, or sometimes nothing at all; but without fail, he was sent away with a happy and hearty "Merry Christmas, Mr. Varney," or hails of "Good tidings" or "Bless you, sir," and many a "Thank you!"

Hank would speak only in mumbled statements like "This'n here," or "Take just a moment in there," or perhaps "Take a bit more time here, if'n you don't mind, Miss Clem," to indicate the location of each intended errand. Otherwise, he went silently about his duties, if indeed that was what they were, zigzagging back and forth across the street and stopping mostly at places Clementine hadn't taken the time before to notice.

As Sol, the Norse goddess of the sun, rode her horse-drawn chariot higher into the sky, Clementine continued to curse her bad luck at not escaping the livery before Jack had found her. Had he known she was prepping Fenrir to leave before walking in on her? If so, how? She'd been so careful and quiet, so sure neither Boone nor Jack had seen her slip into the livery while they unloaded freight. No matter. As soon as Hank was finished with her "help," she would return to the livery for Fenrir and ride out to Slagton.

By mid-morning, Clementine found herself at the edge of Chinatown sitting next to Hank on a portion of porch dry enough not to soak their backsides. Behind them, a haberdashery with coats of wool and leather and horsehair hung behind weepy glass windows. She thought it odd to see such finery in a town that each and every day buried citizens dead of exposure or hunger or the greed of another. Having been Deadwood's sole undertaker until only recently, she knew this notion to be a fact. Thankfully, there was someone else now willing to take in the no-longer-breathing, giving her a much-needed break.

Hank tore apart hunks of jerked beef cured with what he called "dried berry surprise" and handed a piece to Clementine, which made her growling stomach happy. He chewed in silence, his brow furrowed in thought.

Apparently, he'd taken upon himself the task to help those in need; those suffering at the hands of misfortune and foul weather and myriad other burdens laid upon the humanity that populated the Black Hills. Any number of souls would consider it good, gratifying work, yet Hank wore a look of heavy consternation, and that concerned her.

She swallowed a small bite of the salty-sweet jerky. "I knew kindness and empathy were powerful forces in you, Hank, but I had no idea."

His eyes glassed with tears. "It's not enough, Miss Clem. People is sufferin'. Dyin' for want of a decent meal and a warm coat. Good folks, too, most of 'em."

His compassion intrigued her.

For all of her grandparents' strengths and virtues they had shared with Clementine while raising her, they'd taught her naught of sympathy or compassion. Yet she still *felt*—as in a sharp stab of pain through her chest at the worst; and a tightening in her throat at the least. Whether it be for the few friends she had found in her lifetime … and then lost, or the downtrodden workers and scrawny prostitutes of Kongsberg. Or the child laborers in Europe and the industrial centers back east. Or the girls of the line she'd come to know in Deadwood. The sorrow and pity and fury at so much mistreatment burned deep.

Yet, her grandparents had purposely encouraged emotional restraint, even indifference toward others, from the moment they'd taken her in after her mother's brutal murder. Not to be mistaken, Clementine's grandparents were always caring and attentive to her, but they were not what anyone would consider loving or compassionate. They couldn't afford to be, what with tasked in training yet another Slayer; a killer who would be stronger, smarter, and quicker than their previous student—their only daughter, who'd been buried in pieces behind their cottage.

It wasn't until reaching adulthood that Clementine realized her childhood had been methodically constructed with pragmatism and a shrewdness that no doubt kept her in line for the great hall of Valhalla, where only some of the Viking warriors who died in battle were permitted. They had meticulously sculpted her to have a shield of subdued empathy and emotional detachment, which she would need to rely upon continually as a Slayer.

To give proper credit, her grandparents had taught her the duties of her trade well. Most of those she met—human, *other*, or hybrid—elicited little more than indifference from her. This emotional detachment was most likely perceived by those around her as callousness or disgust or a mixture of both. For the most part, Clementine didn't care what they thought. Her purpose in life was set. Until she reached Valhalla, where she would drink to her victories with her fellow warriors, including her mother, she needed to stay the course. Alone.

And she'd been doing just that until lately—fighting alone. She'd learned her lesson the last time she'd let her guard down and allowed someone too close, only to lose them. But then Hank had come along, and a handful of months later, Boone and

Jack, too. Her grasp on indifference had begun to slip yet again, same as before. She cared for these men, and *that* was dangerous. For everyone.

Clementine turned to Hank, suddenly wanting him to know that she understood his compassion. Needing him to see that in spite of how she was raised, no matter how hard she fought it, she still felt emotions.

"I grew up on the shore of the North Sea in Norge," she blurted out. "Norway. Raised by my grandparents, as you know."

His watery gaze shifted to her.

"My mother was killed when I was very young—I think I told you that before." She watched the throng of humanity in the street shuffle, stumble, and trod every which way around them. Many didn't have a coin in their pockets, yet most seemed cheerful, no doubt due to the fact that Christmas was but one day away. "I know nothing of my father. Not even a name. My mother took everything about him to the grave with her."

"You called your grandpappy *afi* and your grammy *amma*, ain't that so, Miss Clem?

"Yes."

"Sad, not knowin' your poppa and momma." He rested his hand on her shoulder. It was oddly comforting, considering that she'd been trained from childhood to snatch, twist, and sometimes break any hand laid upon her.

"I had my amma and afi, though. They lived on a farm, big enough to support the three us, but just barely." She smiled, picturing the green hills of summer sprinkled with wildflowers of yellow, blue, white, pink, and purple. Sweet-smelling memories of rolling around in the meadow behind their barn came and went. "Their cottage was nestled in a small grassy valley between foothills that rose up into tree-covered slopes and rocky cliffs. Those mountains were magnificent to my young eyes. Terrible, menacing, reaching for the clouds with snow-covered, craggy, rocky fingers. In the other direction, the grassy field my grandfather harvested for the animals fell away to the sea. I skittered along behind him on the trail down to the water's edge countless times, winding down to his little skiff. We'd push it into the bay and he'd row us out to fish. I always worried the jagged rocks under the water would gouge a hole in the planks or the keel as we pushed it from the beach, and we'd sink into the dark depths and get gobbled up by *Jörmungandr*."

Hank raised an eyebrow. "Yer-moon what?"

Clementine couldn't help but smile. "Close. He's the son of Loki and Angrboða ..." She trailed off when she noticed his blank stare. "He's a giant sea serpent that could swallow you down his gullet whole."

Hank raised the other eyebrow. "Miss Clem. I've seen some things. Ain't never seen no sea monster, though. Big teeth, I imagine, just like ever' other critter you tend to come up against."

"And don't forget the horns." She stuck both index fingers out from her forehead.

A smile wrinkled the skin around his eyes. "Hoo hoo! Them don't look too bad. Don't amount to no more than puny little fingers." His smile drooped. "Ain't sayin' you got puny little fingers, Miss Clem. Never do that."

Clementine backhanded his shoulder and let out her best imitation of a witch cackle. "I'll hex you with these puny little fingers." She twirled them toward him until he raised his hands in mock fear and shrank back, nearly falling off the porch.

"Turn me to a toad, I expect."

"Or a scaly snake." She pursed her lips, the way she'd seen him do so many times. "Maybe a furry little bunny rabbit."

He snorted. "Jack rabbit."

"Like the wild one back at the livery," she said with a wink.

"Hoo! Somethin', ain't he? I'd just soon not make acquaintance with that Yarmug-dish beasty. Jack Rabbit would likely shake its hand. Or paw, is it?" He scrunched up his face. "What kinda appendages does a sea monster have, you think?

Fishy flippers?"

"Probably enormous claws that grab and squeeze." She snapped at Hank's arm with her clawed hands.

"That's not a comfortin' thought. Wonder if'n a personage could cook it up and eat it." He wrinkled his nose and jiggled his head with a quick shake. "Revoltin' thought." He turned toward her again. "Tell me some more about when you were a young'un. Your little house. Your afi and amma. Catchin' fishies, you say?"

She chewed on her lower lip. There was something about Hank. Something *what*? Disarming? She hadn't spoken to anyone of her childhood much since leaving her grandparents. It'd always been a part of her that she wanted no one to see. Another result of her upbringing, no doubt. She could easily hear the timbre of her afi's voice warning: *Do not allow others to see within you, Liebling. Your thoughts. Your desires. Those are for you alone. They are weaknesses that would be used against you.*

Through her entire childhood, her afi had trained her to bury emotion deep, unexposed to the cruelties of the world. From the sting of a cut finger to the loss of Yrsa, her pet brown bear, to a hunter's arrow.

Your pain must not be displayed. Nor your anger or sadness.

She hadn't been as successful with controlling her temper as she had the other emotions, a point that frustrated her afi to no end. Otherwise, he had been successful in teaching her the fine art of stoicism. Well, mostly.

But Hank ... for a reason she couldn't fathom, she felt compelled to spill truths whenever he asked. What was this power he had over her? It seemed to be loosening her jaw more and more over the months that she had known him.

"No more stories of fishies, then?" Hank broke into her quandary. The image of her afi half-standing in his little boat while flinging a net into the water floated into her thoughts.

"We'd fill the little boat with fish until it was near sinking." The recollection made her throat tighten. For the first in a long time, she felt the old ache again. She missed her afi and amma. And her life with them. "Ah, Hank. How I would love to taste fresh salmon once again. And cod. Herring, too." Memories of her amma's pickled herring on a hunk of cream-soaked bread made her mouth water. She could almost smell it, taste it.

"Fishies. Ain't ate much fishies myself, exceptin' trout. Ain't had those others."

"You'll have to try them sometime."

He nodded, sticking another piece of jerky in his mouth. After a few chews, he asked, "Your afi had cows tho', so that means cheese, right, Miss Clem? Your amma make cheese in that little cottage?"

"Cheese, butter, and more." Her thoughts turned to her amma, who was always busy with the countless responsibilities one has on a small farm. "The farm was remote. Our nearest neighbors were an hour's walk away. A village was a little farther on. We had no horses, only oxen. Cows and goats for milk and cheese and meat. Chickens. A garden."

"Sounds to make a purty picture."

"It was beautiful."

"Did ya do some swimmin' in that big ol' ocean then?"

"The water was much too cold. I did fall in occasionally when my afi rocked the boat while I was retrieving the net or washing my hands." It wasn't until much later that her afi had admitted he'd considered these submersions into the icy cold water as training, in part to learn the skill of swimming, but also to confront her fear of the unknown. Her afi knew that in her mind the darkness of the water concealed all manner of beast. And *Jörmungandr*.

Hank handed her another piece of jerky. "So you didn't have no friends to play with?"

"None. Like I said, neighbors were few and scattered, and most didn't have any children. I later realized my grandparents were particular about the friends they kept." Her amma and afi had made so many sacrifices because of her. She chewed on the jerky, wondering how their life would have been different if Clementine's mother had lived.

"Makes my heart sad for that little Clementine." Hank's shoulders drooped along with the corners of his mouth.

"It wasn't that bad. My grandparents kept me busy." Clementine leaned back on her gloved hands. "I'm sure the isolation was meant to protect me until I was ready to accept the role of Slayer and fend for myself."

"Scared of my own shadow is what I'd be, growin' up like that. Always thinkin' somethin' is gonna jump from behind a tree and kill me."

She shrugged. "It was all I knew. I thought it was the way all kids grew up. One of my very favorite things was to make a boat of bark or leaves and grass and watch it spin and rush down the stream from high up in the hills above the farm all the way to the sea. Yrsa kept me company, too. That was my pet bear we'd found as a cub with a broken leg."

Hank frowned at her. "You had a bear?"

"She was a small bear—probably a runt." Clementine smiled to herself. "After her leg healed, I would run as fast as I could, and she would chase me until she caught me, and then we'd wrestle in the grass or snow. Or I'd hide in the forest. She always found me, though. It was not fair, really, with that big snout of hers." She paused, her eyes growing watery. "Until she was killed." Tears threatened. She dared not look at Hank for fear of losing the battle.

After a couple of hard swallows and a few blinks, she continued. "I weaved some, especially during the long, dark winter nights. There were always weapons to clean and repair, too. Training and more training with my afi. Language lessons with my amma."

She sat upright, swinging her legs so her boot heels thumped lightly against the porch. "It wasn't until years later that my afi started taking me on what he liked to call his *kleine Abenteuer*—his little adventures. That's when I learned more of the world. He would take me into the village to see the people who lived there. There were so many people ... And markets where all manner of peculiar and amazing things were sold."

"But no dances? No shindigs? No family feasts? No Christmas celebrations?"

"We celebrated Christmas, but it was just the three of us. Afi would bring a tree from the forest. We would tie bows to the branches and then light it with candles. It was beautiful." Clementine could picture the scene clearly even after all of these years. "When I was a little older, he took me with him and let me choose the tree. I tried to pick the perfect one, but the trees there always had crooked and twisted branches, or bare patches. Afi said it gave them character." She pulled her coat around her tighter as a cold blast whipped through the gulch. "Amma would bake pork *Ribbe* and cabbage, lutefisk in butter, and boiled cod. Afi would prepare *Smalahove*, but I couldn't stomach watching him pull the skin and meat from a cooked sheep's head." The smell alone had almost put her off the sweets her grandmother baked.

Hank covered his mouth with his hand. "Miss Clem!" He grimaced behind his fingers.

Clementine chuckled and then changed course. "Amma would always bake *Julekake*. That's bread with dried fruit in it. She'd also make *krumkake* and *kransekake*."

Hank watched her, a suspicious look in his eye.

Clementine laughed outright. "Those are sweet treats. Crunchy cookies and cake."

Hank smiled. "Kroom-ka-ka. Krans-ka-ka," he said, trying to repeat her words. "Those sound more to my liking."

"Mine, too. I always miss them come Christmastime."

"You don't have them no more?"

"Not since leaving my grandparents for Germany. I couldn't

find any the way she made them there, at least not in the places I had to go. And there was nobody to share them with, anyway."

"Aww. Now you went an' tugged at my heart again, Miss Clem."

It tugged at her heart, too, darn it. "Should we keep moving? There's still a lot of consignment on good ol' Fred's back. That's what Jack called it, didn't he?"

"Yes, ma'am, he did. And we should get movin'. Lots to do. Get to flappin' my lips and lose track of my errands."

As Hank's stops took them closer to Chinatown, the back of Clementine's neck began to prickle. She didn't go happily into this part of Deadwood.

"Are there any Christmas traditions you like to stick to, Hank?"

He paused for a moment as a train of four men trudged through the muddy snow in front of them carrying an array of burlap sacks and crates destined for a mercantile across the street. After they'd passed, he urged Fred the Mule forward again, telling her, "Ain't never been in a place long enough to call it home, really."

"Jebediah!" A woman's voice pierced the din of the street.

A young boy on the other side of the street shouted back, and then he dashed around them, bumping into Hank, stopping him short. "Sorry, Mr. Hank!" After a nod, he darted off.

"Merry Christmas, young fella. You'da heard me but there you go, 'cross the street already." Hank watched after the boy as he joined an older woman wearing a torn coat with mud coating the hem. She shook her finger at him and then led him inside a store filled with plucked ducks hanging in the window. "Ol' Fred and Hank'd have a condition if they tried to move that fast."

Clementine chuckled as they started down the street again, wondering how the boy knew Hank.

A few steps later, Hank spoke over the street racket, "I reckon Rails and Amelia are somebodies I can spend a Christmas with again."

"You've had Christmas with them in the past?"

"Yes, ma'am. On the railroad." He turned to her, searching for something in her eyes. "I reckon you're tired of railroad stories, though."

"Not at all. I still get a grin when I think about your railroad tale about Banjo. I can just picture that crazy dog riding a horse."

His eyes twinkled. "Hoo! Banjo. He was a character for sure. Always climbin' something, includin' Hades the horse."

"Banjo the climbing canine!" She sidestepped a mash of road apples and yellow snow in the middle of the street.

"Yessir. Wonder about that pup from time to time. 'Course, we got Tinkerdoo, now. She's a ball of verve and vinegar, ain't she?"

"Without a doubt." After crying off and on for days over Yrsa's lifeless body, Clementine had promised herself she'd avoid falling into the trap of caring for animals ever again. But then came Tinker and Fenrir.

Hank directed Fred the Mule around the backside of several buildings toward a log-walled shelter covered with tattered dirty canvas. It was obvious the canvas would do little to keep the cruel, foul Black Hills weather at bay. "Right here, Miss Clem." Hank loosened the rope securing one of the larger bags on Fred's back and pulled it free. "Care to accompany me?"

Clementine thought on it for a moment. It would be simpler to wait. They were still on the fringes of Deadwood's Chinatown, where death dealers such as herself were shunned, and she couldn't be sure who or what she might find inside.

"Come on now, Miss Clem. It won't take but a minute."

Fred the Mule, whether coincidentally or purposely, bumped her toward Hank. While she was getting to know the mule better and better, she couldn't be sure if they were becoming fast friends or just colleagues. Mules were hard to assess that way. Especially Fred.

"Come," Hank insisted.

She obeyed, falling in behind him. After all, how much trouble could come from helping deliver a few supplies?

"Ho there!" Hank bellowed as he approached the pine pole door. "Higginses! Inside!"

The poorly built door swung open. A drooping figure appeared from the shadows. It was a woman, one who couldn't have seen much sleep in days, perhaps weeks. Her scraggly hair was half-covered with a raggedy scarf, her eyes sunken and weary, her face haggard.

"Merry Christmas, Eunice," Hank said, smiling warmly at the frail woman. "How's Lester? Li'l Davey?"

A tired smile was all Eunice gave in return.

Hank hugged her briefly. He had to duck to enter the tiny hut. So did Clementine. She followed Hank dutifully, greeting Eunice with a smile and nod as she passed.

"This here is Miss Clementine Johanssen," Hank proclaimed after Eunice had closed the door behind them. "Won't find a finer woman in the Hills."

"Welcome to our home, Miss Johanssen." Eunice bowed slightly, her weak smile turning into a frown as she glanced around her small, shadow-filled dwelling.

Clementine kept her expression neutral as she took in the square room with a sawdust floor and two pine pole beds covered with layers of linen and muslin and burlap. The room smelled of dirt and unwashed bodies. As she exhaled, her breath steamed in the cold air. The makeshift stove constructed from a coal oil can that sat in the middle of the room was no match for a Black Hills winter day, let alone a frigid night. In fact, Clementine didn't even think there was a fire burning in it until a wisp of smoke escaped and gathered at the apex of the canvas ceiling before escaping out a melon-sized hole cut there.

A staccato of wet coughs emanated from one of the beds.

She squinted into the shadows, catching sight of a dark-haired boy peeking up at her. He was bundled so well in the bed coverings that Clementine hadn't noticed him at first.

"Lester is workin'," Eunice offered and kneeled by the boy's bed, pulling the covers back up over the child's chin. "Won't be home 'til late."

Hank nodded. "Lester is the salt of the earth." He held up the burlap sack he'd taken off of Fred. "In here I got the makin's of a fine Christmas meal." He smiled sadly at Davey. "And some syrup straight from Doc Wahl. Doc said it should help sort out Li'l Davey's cough."

"Bless you, Mr. Varney. Bless you." A tear ran down Eunice's cheek, followed by another before she dabbed at them with the tattered end of her headscarf. "I don't know how we'll repay you."

"None of that now." Hank drew a bottle of dark liquid out of the sack and handed it to Eunice. "Doc Wahl was feelin' particular kind and handed it over straight away with his compliments."

Eunice scoffed. "I know Doc Wahl. He did no such thing." Her gaze narrowed. "He probably charged double just because a body needed it."

Hank scratched at his neck. "Truth be told he is an ornery sort."

Clementine bit back her snort of contempt. It was her experience that Doc Wahl was disagreeable on the best of days.

Davey let fly another series of wet, rattly coughs.

She and Hank watched as Eunice propped the boy to sitting and then spooned a dose of the doctor's tonic into the child's mouth. He sputtered, ejecting a good portion of the liquid onto the dirty blanket covering his chest.

Clementine looked closer at the boy. His appearance overall was wan and gaunt. "May I take a closer look at your son?" she asked his mother.

Eunice glanced up at Hank, concern creasing her brow.

"Miss Clem here knows more about what ails a body, includin' tinctures and balms, than Doc Wahl ever wished he could."

Still frowning, Eunice nodded her consent.

It took but a quick look for Clementine to realize that it was not consumption that distressed the boy, but some form of moist rales. Or maybe worse—some type of lung disease. She picked up the bottle of syrup provided by Doc Wahl and sniffed once. It was nothing more than a little laudanum mixed with some form of alcohol. Sure, it might help quiet the boy, but it would do nothing to help heal him.

Rising, she offered a smile for Eunice before looking at Hank. "I'm ready when you are."

Hank nodded once. "We should be off, Eunice." He turned toward the door. "Ooo! Almost forgot." He pulled a muslin-wrapped packet from his pocket. "This here's for Li'l Davey." He handed the packet to Eunice. "For Christmas."

"Thank you, Mr. Varney," she said, blinking back more tears. "Oh, I have a parcel, too. Can you deliver it to the Williamsons?" Eunice retrieved a paper-wrapped and twine-tied package from a small table next to the other bed. "I knitted a wrap for the baby. I had just enough yarn."

Hank took the small package and patted Eunice on the shoulder. "Good as delivered, don't you fret. Good sentiments to Li'l Davey, there. And Lester and you, too."

"Bless you, Mr. Varney. You are one of God's own."

For the next few deliveries, Clementine accompanied Hank inside the dwellings. To the Williamsons with their almost-new baby. Then into Chinatown to the Changs to deliver a crate to Lao So and his dog, Mika; and to the Wu family with a bag of what smelled like onions. And on and on. Hank seemed tireless, always with plenty of vigor and a heart-lifting smile.

She found that if she kept close to Hank, she was subject to only glimpses of the unpleasant confrontations she had become accustomed to in Chinatown. The glares or verbal slights or physical affronts that inevitably resulted from a female undertaker's unwanted presence only came forth when she strayed from his side for too long. She was beginning to realize that the more she learned of Hank the less she knew of him.

By midday, they were back at the edge of Chinatown where the cultures and customs of different people blended together. Fred the Mule's load had been reduced to one burlap sack regardless of the fact that they had picked up many packages as they traveled. Clementine and Hank found a makeshift bench and sat for a rest away from the clamor of a street filled with those preparing for the holiday.

As she chewed on another hunk of Hank's jerky, Clementine decided that she quite liked meat cured with "dried berry surprise." It brought warmth to her belly, whether real or imagined. The steaming canteen of hot tea Hank had been given at their last stop was helping to heat up the rest of her in spite of the crisp, face-numbing weather.

"Looky there, Miss Clem." Hank nodded up the street toward Deadwood proper where a group of fancy-dressed *hens* strutted along the boardwalk. The women's wool hats were embellished with bright green and red dyed feathers that bobbed with each step as they clucked and laughed and pecked along. Occasionally, they'd stop in front of a shop window and pull their hands from their thick fur muffs to point at whatever they saw—probably a colorful set of china, or a bow-and-lace-covered bonnet, or a bolt of satin or silk fabric. Clementine would have rather spent her time staring into the new confectionery store's window just down from The Pyre at the beautiful Christmas cakes and frosting-lined gingerbread cookies.

"Picking out Christmas gifts looks like," Hank said. "Happy as bugs in a warm bed." His cheerful smile landed on her. "Do your feelin's run that way? Or would you just as soon head for Slagton this very minute?"

Clementine chewed for a moment, pondering her answer. For the better part of the morning, Hank had occupied her to the edge of distraction. At several points, the thought had crossed her mind to cut from Hank and head out, but he always seemed to especially need her help at just those times. Coincidence or something else, she couldn't be sure. But the task that awaited her in Slagton continued to lurk at the edge of her thoughts.

"As soon as you no longer need my help here, Hank, I'll be on my way."

Hank sobered. "I see."

She stared down the street, back toward Chinatown, taking in all of the bulbous colorful paper lanterns that hung from the storefronts down that way. "It's not that—"

"I have a Christmas present for you," he interrupted, hopping off the bench to fetch the last paper-wrapped package from the burlap sack hanging from Fred's back. He returned and handed it to her. "Merry Christmas, Miss Clem. I was hopeful I'd get to give you that tomorrow before Christmas supper, but that don't sound like a possibility, so …"

Clementine turned the package this way and that, examining the work put into it. "It's a beautiful bow, Hank."

"Thank you, Miss Clem. Tied it myself."

Verdammt. The glassiness in Hank's gaze had returned. He looked away quickly, focusing down the street, and swiped across his eyes with his sleeve. "Sure is purty, all those lanterns. Come nighttime, they light 'em all with candles. Sorry to say you'll miss it. It is a sight to behold." He snorted but kept his face turned away from her.

"Shall I open it now?"

"It's yours to do with." He wandered over to Fred and stroked his neck.

She wasn't sure of the etiquette concerning Christmas presents. She'd not received one in so long. "Hank, earlier you mentioned that you'd enjoyed spending Christmas with Mr. Beaman and Amelia. Can you tell me about that Christmas?"

"Surely." A hint of smile ghosted his face as he returned and settled down on the bench next to her again. "If they's ever a pair what knows how to host a party, it's them two." He held his hands up in front of his chest as if he were holding a box, bringing his arms and hands into the conversation. "Now see, Amelia, she does the decoratin'. Silk bows or purty-colored linen bows and garlands and bunches of sage and other purty bouquets she gets her little hands on. That's what she did when we was on the railroad." He sat up straighter. "We was livin' in tents is all, but they was homes to us. We worked all day, yet Amelia scraped up the time to gather dried flowers and garlands and such. Hung it all in their tent."

"It sounds beautiful." His description reminded her a little of her grandparents' house at Christmastime.

He nodded animatedly. "And Rails, he forged up little metal ornaments and hung 'em in the Christmas tree with twine. Holders for the candles. Stars and bears and birds and, well, all manner of fancy hangin' things." Hank gazed at Fred, looking lost in memory. "Beautiful blacksmithin', it was. At the end, he gave 'em all away, every last one. Still got a little bow made of metal." He grinned her way. "Ever heard of such a thing? Bow made of metal?"

"Never. How did he have time to do that? It must have been a lot of work."

"Yes, ma'am. I think he worked on them little trinkets all year and saved 'em up."

"So, I'm guessing all of this preparing and decorating wasn't for just the three of you?"

"Oh noooo. End of the evening, pert near the whole camp had been in that little tent, bringin' whatever they could. Roast rabbit or chicken. Boiled potatoes. Some even brung a pie or two. Beer. Cider. And for those that was in need, socks and britches and boots. All things of that sort. Ever'body sharin' and laughin' and dancin'. Fiddler and banjo man a-playin' into the night. Hoo hoo! It was a shindig to beat all."

"The Beamans did all this?" They didn't seem the revelry sort of folk. Both had plenty of smiles to spare, yet were always hard at work every time she saw them.

"Yes, ma'am."

"The same Beamans now living and employed at the livery?"

"The very same."

Now that she thought about it, Amelia had mentioned that she was interested in decorating the livery for Christmas. The girl was probably doing that very thing right now in between taking care of the animals.

"You ever been to a shindig like that, Miss Clem? Prob'ly not, huh? I'd expect you to be more of the cup-of-tea-alone-by-the-fire type."

Anymore, that was true, but there was a time when she'd tried to blend with the local community and culture. In fact, there had been a period of time when she desperately wanted to belong. To associate with others and experience companionship. Friendship. Intimacy. All of it. And forsake her purpose in life.

To that end, she'd acquiesced to something her amma had warned to avoid at all costs. She'd taken a lover.

It had begun innocently on her part, not long after her seventeenth year. She had struck out into the world and found a comfortable niche in a small German village employed as a baker's assistant. She had not yet been called upon to perform her duties as a Slayer and found life somewhat leisurely and unencumbered.

"Miss Clem?" Hank was watching her.

"What? Oh." Clementine shook the memories from her head.

"Recollectin'? See it in your eyes."

"I suppose."

"Folks? Or things?"

"A little of both. People mostly. One in particular." She studied Hank, knowing she should change the subject, but for some reason unable to keep from divulging. "His name was Andreas."

"Andreas. Handsome name. A friend back in the old country then?" Hank leaned in closer.

"He was ... my first suitor." She sighed, aiming a half-hearted scowl at Hank. "By Odin's one eye! What is it about you that makes a person tell you their most private thoughts?"

He shrugged and a smile crept onto his face. "It certainly causes difficult conditions in my conversatin' from time to time. Distressin' even. Not for me, mind you." He squinted at the sky. " 'Ceptin' that one time." He shook his finger in the air. "Didn't want nothin' to do with seein' her bloomers. Wasn't in my collection of wants and desires, rest assured."

Clementine let out a bark of laughter. "Whose bloomers are you talking about?"

"Oh, uh ..." Hank stared down at his hands, his cheeks flushed. "So, Andreas. *Inamorato,* was he?"

"Lover? Yes." She sniffed, dabbing her cold nose with the back of her glove, and then continued with her tale. "The village I was staying in was celebrating the *große Ernte,* the Grand Harvest, a week-long autumn festival where bread, cheese, and meat were plentiful; music, singing, and dancing were nonstop; and beer flowed freely."

She toyed with the twine on Hank's Christmas present. "It was my first experience with alcohol other than the mead my afi would make. And my first experience with a man. Andreas was ..." She trailed off, smiling at the memory of his charming smile and expert touch. She cleared her throat, moving onward with her tale. "He was the perfect gentleman through and through. We grew close over the following winter and talked of many things—food, music, dreams, the future." Clementine's gaze drifted over the crowd of shoppers and miners, pausing on a group of carolers singing a tune that she couldn't quite make out. "There was even mention of marriage."

But she'd been young and naïve, ignoring her amma's warning.

"Didn't come to America, though," Hank said quietly.

"No. He didn't." The sting of pain was still there. It continued to mellow with time, but never fully eased.

Hank gave her a sideways hug and then pointed at the paper-wrapped package in her hands. "Care to gander?"

Blinking away the past, she pulled on the neatly tied twine bow. "You wrapped this?"

Hank nodded once and dawned a satisfied smile. "My pleasure for you, Miss Clem."

She freed the package from the twine and carefully unwrapped the paper. She gasped, holding up a silk chemise embroidered with a multi-colored dragon swirled from the hem up around the back to a gaping maw under the neckline.

"Oh, Hank," she said under her breath. She tugged off one of her gloves and ran her fingers over the cool fabric. It was so soft and shiny. The dragon needlework was amazingly detailed. She'd never seen such a divine chemise.

A loud whinny followed by a volley of curses in the street jerked her out of her trance. She quickly folded away the chemise and wrapped the paper around it before glancing around at the passersby. Thankfully, nobody had noticed her oohing and ahhing about her unmentionables in the street.

She reached out and caught Hank's hand. "It's extraordinarily beautiful, Hank. It must be what it's like to touch a cloud. Thank you."

Hank grinned, his pink cheeks darkening once again. "Figured I was takin' a chance on inpurtenance. But knowin' you and your predilection for silk, well, I squashed the inappropriate nature of the gift. You sure you like it?"

"I do." She chuckled, squeezing his hand. "I'm glad you did 'squash the inappropriate nature.' It's lovely and I can't wait to try it on." She tied the twine around the package, but not quite so neatly as Hank had.

"If you'd like, I'll have Fred carry that back to The Pyre for ya, Miss Clem. Sure glad you like it."

She leaned over and dropped a kiss on his cheek, surprising him judging by his suddenly wide eyes.

"Aw, Miss Clem. Don't go gettin' yer lips tainted on my dirty ol' face." He blushed even deeper red and his eyes grew watery yet again.

"There could be a layer of mud on your cheek, Hank, and I'd still kiss you for that thoughtful gift."

Hank sniffed. "I think you're one of the best of folks I ever met, Miss Clem, and I consider myself damn lucky to know ya." He toed at a chunk of ice near his foot, swiping at his eyes. "We should mosey afore you get me to blubberin' about it."

She laughed. "Okay, okay. Are we finished with our deliveries?"

"Not ever, really, but for now. Gotta head on. I'll walk you to the livery. I reckon you're still bent on Slagton as a destination today, even though it's the eve of Christmas and the fact that your companions—bein' me and the Sidewinders—just might enjoy spendin' Christmas Day with you don't matter much when you got important things that need tendin' …" He took a breath. "… when we was happy, might say eager, to lend a hand to a companion such as yerself, but if yer itchn' to git kilt even if we was to foller along …" He took another breath, but then paused to glance at her. "Be in a person's mind to help a friend is all I'm sayin', since that's what people do when they see somethin' needs doin' and it bein' Christmas and all we—"

"Hank." She crossed her arms.

"… thought a nice Christmas supper to send us, all of us, on out to Slagton on a full belly day after Christmas maybe and then—"

"Hank!" she said, a little louder this time.

"Yes, ma'am." Hank pulled off his hat and held it in front of his belly, staring down at the ground like a scolded puppy.

"We should head toward the livery." It was midday now, and while there was no way to make it to Slagton before sundown, she still wanted to be on her way.

With a nod, he led the way up the street at a frustratingly slow pace. When Clementine suggested picking up the pace, Hank blamed Fred the Mule for his lack of gumption.

"You'll tell me more about Andreas sometime, Miss Clem," Hank stated rather than asked as he tugged on Fred's lead rope to slow him down even more.

When they approached the front of the livery, Clementine caught sight of a familiar, bearded blond troublemaker sitting up on a partially loaded freight wagon.

"Heyo, Jack Rabbit!" Hank called up at him. He swished Fred the Mule into a hasty clip to meet his friend.

"Hanky Panky," Jack greeted in return, his grin wide as he climbed down to join them. "Lost your consignment, I see." Jack patted Fred's haunch and then looked Clementine over. "Not all of it, though. Still got a little baggage to deliver."

"Mr. Jack Fields," Clementine scolded with a smile and poked his arm. "Are you saying I'm nothing more than a trunk of meaningless belongings?"

Jack shrunk away, rubbing his arm. " 'Course not. You'd never fit in a trunk with those legs."

This time she punched him in the arm.

"Ow!" He rubbed his arm harder. "I'm just sayin' Hank tends to pick up this-n-that off the street and bring it home."

She opened her mouth wide in mock disbelief. "Well, I never!" Then she ruined it by bursting into laughter.

Jack joined her merriment while still massaging his arm. After they quieted, he slapped Hank on the back. "Well, old man." He leaned closer and whispered loudly near Hank's ear, "So far so good." After giving Hank a wink, he turned back to Clementine. "I got a little problem, Miss Clementine."

"You haven't really studied the art of subtlety, have you, Jack?" Even an imbibed dullard could guess their game. "You intend to delay me, right? As in sabotage, pure and simple. Or in pirate parlance, you intend to waylay me."

"Miss Clementine," Jack said, his eyes sparkling. " 'Waylay' isn't a pirate word."

" 'Shanghai,' then?"

"That one is. But I don't mean to shanghai you so much as waylay you." Jack grinned at her.

"You're a scalawag, Jack 'Rabbit' Fields."

"Arrgh. Sink me, lassie. No need to toss shark bait in me mizzen." Jack squinted up with one eye mostly closed and grit his teeth.

"How's that now, Jack Rabbit?" Hank scratched his jaw.

"Never mind, Hank." Jack straightened up. "Miss Clementine, I need your help. Won't take long and then you can be on your way."

Clementine frowned up at the clear blue sky. Sol and her chariot had reached the apex of her daily race across the heavens. She really needed to hit the trail.

With a sigh, she looked back. "What do you need, Jack?"

STAVE THREE

*The Second
of the Three Friends*

"Let's be clear on something, Jack," Clementine aimed a narrow-eyed glare at Rabbit. "I'm not going to follow you all over Deadwood for half the day. If your intent is to 'waylay' me further, I fear your disposition will suffer greatly in the revelation of your failure."

Rabbit grimaced. "Miss Clementine, you're soundin' more like Booney day by day." His *compadre* had been spouting big, fancy-sounding words ever since Uncle Mort had brought home a crate of old books he'd won in a card game back when Rabbit and Boone were still trying to catch lizards for fun.

Her squint deepened. "You might as well cash in your chips on this hand and let me head for Slagton now."

"Say, you hear about the Christmas parade planned for tomorrow afternoon?" He hopped across a trench zigzagging down and across the street, half-filled with muddy runoff. Rabbit's hope that it was mud was belied by the nauseating odor wafting up from it and clinging to the inside of his nose. He offered a hand to Clementine, which she immediately batted away. She leapt over to him effortlessly and brushed her hands down her trousers and wool coat.

"Like a deer." Rabbit grinned.

He'd be happy as a card sharp holding a full house to pull up a chair and watch the "Amazon" do anything she cared to— dispatch in grand fashion a *Bahkauv* or three; lope up the livery loft steps two at a time on those looong legs; ride Fenrir, her shiny black oversized Morgan; or maybe just stroll down the street, swinging that long, auburn braid. Clementine was a sight Rabbit hadn't yet grown tired of, and probably wasn't likely to either.

"What are we about today, Jack?" Her cheeks were pink with cold, along with her nose.

"Uhhh. What now, Miss Clementine?" He tipped his hat at a pair of fine-looking ladies dressed in pretty green and blue velvet gowns with matching smocks, muffs, and hats, earning a couple of shy smiles in return.

"Judging by your lackadaisical gait," Clementine said, matching his pace, "I'd guess that you are feeling especially leisurely this morning."

"Aw, I don't know about that. Enjoyin' a turn with my favorite *amiga* is what I'd call it."

Rabbit ambled along as slowly as he reckoned he could get away with, tipping his hat several more times, shouting out holiday greetings to familiar faces, pausing to peer in a store window or two. Anything he could do to slow Clementine down. The way he figured, Hank had probably run out of distractions and that was why he'd circled around to the livery again.

"*Amiga.* Is that what I am?" She leaned into a gust of cold air that had them both tightening their collars. "I like the sound of that, Jack. So, if a friend is a man, he's an *amigo*, right?"

"*Sí, señorita.*"

"And that means a young, unmarried woman?"

"*Sí, señorita*," he repeated, adding a wink.

"*Bueno, amigo.* But I'm not so young anymore." She adjusted her scarf. "Men are o's and women are a's, is that it?"

"A little more to it than that, but you get the notion." It sounded strange to hear Clementine speaking Spanish. He'd become accustomed to her swearing in Norse, or Norwegian, or whatever she called it. That and German, which Rabbit had heard plenty of around Deadwood. It didn't mean he understood one any better than the other, but Spanish he'd grown up around. "*Eres una buena amiga.*"

She looked over at him with a wrinkled brow. "What's that mean?"

"You're a good friend."

She stopped. Her smile reached clear up to her eyes. "*Eres

una buena amigo."

"Close," he said with a grin. "It would be, '*Eres un buen amigo.*' You have to take the 'a' off *una* and *buena* to make it masculine."

"No 'o' this time except for the end. That's tricky."

"Yep."

"*Eres un buen amigo,* Jack."

He watched her for a moment, letting his grin fade. "I'm heartened to hear that, Miss Clementine. Boone and me, we've taken a real likin' to you."

"Likewise," she said with a wrinkle on her brow, looking a slight bit unhappy about the matter.

Rabbit started strolling up the street again. "I been doin' some thinking."

"Uh oh."

"Stop it, wiseacre." He used his boot to push a loose plank over a particularly large slushy patch of mud so that Clementine could avoid stepping in it. "Boone and me, we know you've been on your own most of your life. A lone wolf. Don't need no pack. We didn't neither, really. Been side by side since we were young'uns and didn't see no need for no one else. We know people, sure, but they ain't normally the kinda people you put to your back in a fight. 'Acquaintances,' Boone calls 'em.'" He sidestepped a scrawny man with a long scraggly beard tottering along, catching a strong whiff of alcohol from him. "You and Hank," he continued when she was back at his side. "You two are different. The kinda people we want to watch out for. It ain't nothin' you plan for, it kinda just happens." He nodded at a familiar-looking man in a fur hat as he passed. "You probably don't know what I'm talking about, huh, Miss Clementine?"

He'd gone several steps before realizing that Clementine had stopped again.

When he halted and looked back, she was studying him with her head tipped slightly. After a moment, she pointed at him.

"You don't want me to go to Slagton alone, but you're not too good at saying it flat out."

"Well, I can go get Boone if you want to hear him prattle on about it. He'll talk your ear off with his considerations, and he'll use bigger words in the tellin'."

She chuckled, staring back toward the livery with a soft gleam in her eyes. "That man does ponder a point to the very end, doesn't he?"

"Ruminates more than a cow in a field of dry grass is what he does. Drives me to distraction on occasion."

"Me, too," she said, her expression sobering. She pulled him just inside the alley between a café and its neighboring dry goods store.

As soon as they were more or less alone, she continued, "Well, Jack, you're not wrong. I am wholly accustomed to working alone. For years I've been responsible for myself and only myself, whether it be while wandering from place to place or fighting for my life. But within the last few months, I find myself preoccupied with not one, but three new acquaintances who insist on tending to *my* responsibilities." She touched her palm to her chest, adding emphasis. "Besides the fact that I'm far from comfortable with the notion of having to confer with a committee before making a decision, do you have any idea how I'd feel if any of you were injured or killed because of me?"

Rabbit actually had given her reluctance to include them a moderate amount of thought. "I thought you Viking sorts believe your death has been settled on already and there's no changin' the date."

"Well, yes, however—"

"I know, I know. You like to howl at the moon alone anyhow."

She scowled, chewing on her lower lip. "I'm going to be honest with you right now, Jack. Do you remember what happened in Galena?"

"Who wouldn't?"

"Do you recall a knife to your ribs?"

"It mighta seemed that way, but—"

"Mm hmm." She cut him off. "While I helped you remain un-skewered, a certain menace escaped my grasp."

Rabbit remembered exactly what happened and had dragged himself through hot coals about it ever since. "Bad luck was all. That won't—"

"Do you remember what happened in the cemetery?" She planted her hands on her hips.

"Sure do. I dropped ..." he paused to count on his fingers. "Six or seven of those *caper-sus* rascals, I think."

"Rascals" was too nice a name for those mush-headed menaces with their telltale goat-pig tattoo—or branding scar or ring—that showed off their allegiance to a bunch of nasty sons-a-bi ... blunderbusses. He could think of plenty of other more appropriate names to give them no-good scoundrels, being that they were bent on building an army of troublemakers set on taking over Deadwood and the rest of the Black Hills while wiping out Clementine in the process. But being it was Christmas Eve, a particular time of the year when Uncle Mort was apt to make Rabbit and Boone lug extra loads of firewood if they were caught swearing, he was trying to curb his colorful language some.

"Four *caper-sus*," Clementine said. "You dropped four. And that's not what I'm talking about." She exaggeratedly rubbed her shoulder where her enemy's sword had stuck fast into her scapula that night in the cemetery.

"Oh. Yeah. I'm not sure *that*," he said, pointing at her shoulder, "was my fault." But if he were honest with himself, guilt was eating him up about that, too.

Her brow tightened.

"Okay, okay." He held his palms out, deflecting her glare.

She rubbed the back of her neck, frowning toward the main

street. "There have been times Boone has been a distraction, too."

"Ain't gonna argue with you there. He taxes a temperament, to be sure." He chuckled a little, only to quiet when she didn't join him.

When her gaze returned to his, she was dead serious. "So, perhaps you can explain to me what ignorance would justify the added burden of worrying about the two of you when I'm fighting for my life? And make no mistake, that's exactly the situation in Slagton—life or death."

A strong gust whooshed down the alley, making them hold onto their hats.

After it passed, she pulled out her kerchief and dabbed at her nose. "Listen, Jack, after some thought I have decided it would be much safer for the three of you to stay in Deadwood and see to your own business rather than risk your lives dealing with *other*-related things that don't concern you."

Rabbit's face warmed. His chest grew tight, making it more and more difficult to breathe, until it felt like a big old rock was sitting on it.

Justify the added burden ... She had cut to the quick of it, as precise and deadly with her words as she was with her weapons.

He took a step back, stinging from her sharp tongue. All of this arguing with her was starting to feel pointless. In fact, he reckoned he understood her point of view real clear now.

"We never wanted to be a *burden*, Miss Clementine." His lips were stiff from more than the cold. "If that's how you feel, you might just as well head on to Slagton. Don't let me slow you down no more."

He'd be damned if he were going to stick around being some kind of liability. Without another word, he returned to the main street and went on his way, slowing to sidestep a pair of men who were stove-round in the middle and in the midst of discussing the goings-on planned for Christmas. Their bulbous bellies jiggled when they burst into laughter over a joke Rabbit didn't catch.

"Jack!" Clementine's voice pierced through the crowd of people rushing every which way.

He didn't bother to look back. The stubborn woman couldn't have made it any clearer—she considered them a burden. Friends, sure, but a burden still.

"To hell with Slagton," he growled, picking up his pace. "I got things to do."

Everyone around him seemed to be in a jolly mood, even those who were busy doing things they did every day. Why in the world would anyone be happy sweeping a boardwalk or carrying firewood or doing whatever mundane thing that needed doing? Why so many darn smiles?

Christmas is all? Bah.

At the moment he couldn't muster even a smirk.

Ignorance. Bah.

Burden? He grunted. *Fine! Have it your way.*

His stride lengthened and quickened even more. His anger and disappointment drove him to Yellow Strike Saloon in no time, in spite of the inordinate number of citizens strolling along apparently without a care to "burden" their thoughts.

Rabbit shoved open the doors to the saloon and sauntered inside, not really feeling like sauntering at all.

"Gentleman Jack Fields!" Porter the bartender called in his typical carnival barker tone. "Welcome back to Yellow Strike."

Rabbit's disposition instantly improved a little. He actually had a purpose for being at this saloon today.

And a beer wouldn't hurt none either.

He bellied up to the bar. "Barkeep! Squeeze some gold dust from that greasy mop on your head and buy me a barleycorn!"

Rabbit and Boone had met Porter awhile back on their first day in Deadwood when they'd come looking for Uncle Mort. It turned out the barkeep wasn't a particularly likable sort, as in not real trustworthy or affable. But he wasn't necessarily a bad bloke either, so long as an *hombre* didn't turn his back on him.

"Girls are ready, just like you asked, Mr. Fields." Porter pulled a mug full of beer and set it in front of Rabbit.

"Good. Hand me that crate back there, then give the bell a yank."

Porter hefted a crate onto the bar and clanged the bell. "They'll be down directly."

"You are a nobleman and have my gratitude, good sir." Rabbit bowed gallantly. Then he grabbed the mug of beer, clunked it on the crate, and gingerly carried both over to an empty table so as not to slosh beer over the sides. There were only a handful of others keeping Porter company at the moment, and the lot of them were too busy with their faces planted in their cards to pay him any mind.

As he set the crate down, in the periphery of his vision he noticed a certain tall woman, dressed more or less like a man, enter the saloon and situate herself at a table near the door. He avoided looking directly at her and gulped the entire beer without taking a breath. He didn't know what Clementine was doing in the saloon, and he wasn't interested in asking.

"Don't want to be an ignorant burden," he grumbled and pulled the lid from the crate, flinging it into the corner.

"If it isn't Mr. Jack Fields!" called out a sultry, raspy voice from the balcony. "The handsomest *bandito* in the whole of the Dakota Territory."

Rabbit looked up to see a flock of doves lining up along the railing next to Mollie Johnson, the madam. His gaze dipped southward of the madam's brightly painted lips, centering on the very low neckline of her frilly pink dress. "Mollie and her humongous—" He squeezed his lips together when he realized he was talking out loud. At Mollie's arched brow, he finished with, "Heart."

Her smile widened. "You don't say?"

Donning a wide grin of his own, he added, "I don't know about bein' the handsomest in the whole territory, Miss Mollie. Maybe just the Black Hills."

Mollie let out a bark of laughter, then waved the girls to follow her and started down the staircase.

"Hello, ladies!" Rabbit grabbed the hat from his head and held it up in greeting.

As the pretty ladies jiggled and wiggled down the stairs after Mollie, a barrage of greetings the likes of "Hello, Jack," and "Good to see you, JR," and "Howdy, Mr. Sidewinder," filled the saloon.

Rabbit moved to the foot of the staircase, lending the madam a hand. "Miss Mollie." He bowed, sparing only the slightest of glances at her extra-voluptuous attributes before moving on to the next girl.

He chatted with each one as they stopped at his side and patted his chest or gave him a quick kiss or squeezed his ... cheeks. As in the topside ones, not the bottom. Well, mostly topside. They were mighty friendly girls, after all.

"Hello, Maisy. Pearl. Rose." And then, "I'm sorry, sugar, I don't remember your name." Followed by, "That's a pretty ribbon, Squeaky." And finally, "Fannie, still bulging in all the right places, I'm glad to see. Oh, and Fancy's here, too. You shave those toes yet, darlin'?" That last bit earned him a squeal of laughter and a playful swat.

The women gathered around him at the table with the crate, giggling and tittering until Rabbit rapped his knuckles on the wood to quiet them. "Happy to see you all here, and a merry Christmas to you!"

A round of "Merry Christmas" was returned.

"I won't take your time." He knew the girls were on the clock and Angus Monty, the owner of Yellow Strike, was the man watching that clock. Then again, to hell with Angus. He was an ill-tempered, irritable man and ran his saloon like a tight-fisted, below-the-belt-hitting swindler. Girls of the line included. "Or maybe I will."

Rabbit had made no attempt prior to today to conceal his contempt for Monty, nor had Monty disguised his detestation of Rabbit, especially after a certain Sidewinder shot and killed the fancy—and expensive—chandelier that once graced the rafters of Yellow Strike. That chandelier had been replaced by a somewhat less impressive candle wheel hanging from a simple rope and pulley contraption. Undoubtedly, Monty would be perfectly happy to string Rabbit up with that very same rope, but Monty held a grudging respect for Rabbit's trigger finger. And fists. Twice since the death of the chandelier Rabbit had laid out a big man with a bigger mouth at Yellow Strike, and Monty had been there to watch. It gave Rabbit no small amount of satisfaction to know that the rotten son of a gun steamed his collar every time Rabbit entered his establishment, but was too frightened to throw him out.

All the same, Rabbit had gone easy on the foul-tempered tightwad. Since Rabbit had begun frequenting Yellow Strike, there had been no stories of abuse of the girls by Monty or the rest of the employees at the saloon. Rabbit had seen to that himself. He could still picture the wide-eyed look on Monty's face when Rabbit had told the owner, "You beat one more girl, your head rolls next."

Movement across the room drew his gaze. Clementine was watching him openly, but her face was as unreadable as a plank of wood. What was she doing here? It couldn't be out of remorse for her earlier words. That wasn't usually her way.

Burden. Ignorant.

His chest tightened. Those two words were really stuck in Rabbit's craw.

Shaking off his tension, he peered down at the ladies surrounding him. They looked sickly. Malnourished or slaked with opium. Pale. Worn out. And just plain defeated. Damn this town and its brutality. These girls had been beaten like rugs on Sunday, their spirits had been broken and cast aside, but they still had smiles to wear for him.

Rabbit had learned long ago from Uncle Mort that it was the simplest of acts that most sustained the spirit. An unexpected kindness. A thoughtful word or a compassionate gesture, especially in a town that ground the life out of so many.

These women had been shown no charity of any kind. When Rabbit realized the indecency of it, he'd decided he would try to tip the scale, if only a little, away from malicious disregard and want. Tip it toward charity, fortune, and contentedness for those who strived for it but found themselves lacking.

"You brought us gifts?" Mollie asked, peeking into the crate. "What a sweet gentleman you are!"

"A little somethin' to keep your parts warm on long Deadwood nights." He pulled a pair of red flannel unders from the crate and held them up. "Looks like these are for Rose."

Rose cried out, hugged him, and grabbed the long flannels, holding them up and smooshing them against her face. "They're sooo soft and warm. Thank you thank you thank you, Mr. Fields!"

"You are welcome, little Rose." Rabbit grinned as the warmth of her delight blanketed him.

He continued pulling sets of red flannels from the crate and handing them out to the grateful girls until a train of four brown- and white-clad men burst through the front door carrying armloads of goods.

"Great!" Rabbit clapped his hands once. "Dinner is here."

Each of the four men was laden to the point of grunting as they set their baskets and crates onto two tables Porter quickly shoved together. First came a keg and a giant pot, its contents steaming up toward the rafters. Next came several types of cheese and smoked meats, along with pickled eggs and bread. And last, the muslin was pulled from a large metal tray to reveal two roasted turkeys with all of the fixings around them. The delicious aroma of meat drifted through the saloon.

Rabbit grinned wide at the spread of food that he'd ordered compliments of Dmitry and Alexey, two of his friends who worked in the kitchen at The Dove—the finest bathhouse and brothel in Deadwood. The twin Russians had outdone themselves this time. When he'd told the two about the reprehensible treatment the girls of the line at Yellow Strike endured on a daily basis, they were only too happy to grant Rabbit's wish of a few vittles for a Christmas dinner. Only this wasn't a few vittles. This was the kind of *fiesta* he'd expect of Uncle Mort if he were still alive.

Rabbit would doubly need to thank Dmitry and Alexey, and Madam Hildegard, too, for that matter. The proprietor of The Dove surely knew about this, as none of it could have happened without her approval. Although Rabbit did suspect those two Russians could be extremely persuasive when given the motivation to be.

Barkeep Porter dropped a handful of forks and stack of tin plates on the turkey table and then lingered, licking his chops. Rabbit watched him with a hard squint until the barkeep returned to his position behind the counter. A glance toward the corner found those men still mostly focused on their game.

"All right, ladies," he said, turning to the girls. "Grab a fork and load your plates. All this food is for you."

As the girls moved toward the food, Rabbit kept glancing between the barkeep and the top of the stairs. If Angus Monty was fool enough to come out of his room and down those stairs, well, he might have to …

"Oh, Mr. Rabbit Fields! You are simply the kindest, most thoughtful man I've ever laid eyes on." Maisy, the shortest and skinniest girl in the group, jumped up and locked her arms around Rabbit's neck, her feet dangling well off the ground. "I don't know how to thank you." She kissed his cheek several times.

Rabbit laughed down at her. "How old are you, Maisy?"

She smiled dreamily back at him. "I don't know. Madam Mollie thinks I'm probably fourteen or fifteen." She let go of his neck and dropped to the floor.

So young! Angus Monty should be strung up by his balls. "You're welcome more than I can say, darlin'. Now, go get yourself a plate of turkey."

Fourteen or fifteen. Rabbit glared at the door at the top of the stairs again. He mustered just enough gumption to keep himself from stomping up those steps, kicking in Monty's door, and wringing the life from the wretched man. His fingers brushed over the knife sheathed on his belt. Maybe …

No. Not today. Today was for celebrating. Besides, Yellow Strike Saloon now had a good woman in Madam Mollie. She cared for these girls almost as much as Madam Hildegard cared for hers. Angus Monty's time was coming. But today, he could wait.

"What's this, Jack?" Mollie held up a mug then pointed at the keg with it. "It's as fine as any wine I've ever tasted, but it's different."

"It's mead." Rabbit's taste for mead was as strong as his taste for tequila. But mead was even harder to come by. When Alexey said he would deliver a barrel of mead to the Jack Fields Feast, Rabbit had given the Russian a neck squeeze along the likes of Maisy's. Only he'd spared Alexey the kisses, not wanting to incite the big Russian one way or another.

"Mead? It's delightful!" Mollie took another gulp. "Sweet, like apple juice, but with a bite, like beer."

"It's made from fermented honey. I think I'll try a bit myself." The server pouring the elixir into tin cups overheard and offered one to Rabbit.

In his exuberance to taste it, he poured a little more than enough into his mouth. It coated his tongue and warmed his throat as it made its way down to his belly. The sweet complex flavor reminded him of some of the tonics he'd tried on his travels with Boone over the years while freighting goods from this city to that. But it was better, like everything the Russian twins did. He took another sip, basking in the girls' merriment.

Within no time, all of the girls were laughing and dancing and eating. Fancy and Fannie shooed away the piano player and started in on a melody Rabbit didn't recognize:

Ohhhhh,
Won't someone bring me the manniest maaan
That will be more than happy to fill up my caaan
(with money)
He'll buy me frilly French dresses
And clean up my messes
or at least put some meat in my fryin' paaan
(-taloons).

They both took healthy swigs of mead from their cups and then continued ...

Ohhhhh,
Welllll,
We might as well make him a Dandy
With big bags of jewels and sweet Candy
He'll come teach those bad Miners
That there's nothin' finers
Than girls with round apples and fine fanny
(-ssssss).

Ohhhhh,
If miners and cowboys get mean,
My man who has muscles so lean
Will take his big stick
And beat the mean ...

They both took another swig.

♪ *... bloodsucking tick*
An' then tend to his oh so sweet queen

Squeaky joined them when they started all over again.

Ohhhhhh,
Won't someone bring me the manniest maaan ... ♪

Madam Mollie touched his shoulder, pulling his attention away from the piano. "We won't ever know how to thank you, Jack." Her smile had a touch of sadness as she watched the girls flitter about, giggling and twirling.

Her touch warmed his heart even more. After Maisy's sweet thank you and all of the girls' jollity, Rabbit reckoned he might be glowing from the inside out. Their good cheer had him smiling wider than ever.

"This is the thanks right here." Rabbit swept his hand through the air, and then he looked up at Mollie. "You and these girls got a lousy row to hoe. Full of rocks, my uncle would say. Well, I'm gonna help to move some of those rocks out of your way."

Mollie's eyes filled with tears.

"Don't go doin' that now, Miss Mollie." He took her hand and squeezed it. "You need more mead."

Grabbing her cup, he started for the keg. On the way, he glanced at Porter behind the bar. The barkeep was silent, watching the party. If his face drooped any more, it might drip clean down to the floor and puddle there with the nose sticking up. The sight of the pitiful wretch plucked at Rabbit's heartstrings.

Porter wasn't evil, though he worked for a man who was. Many of the girls working in various Deadwood saloons and brothels had been shanghaied or tricked into coming to this town, and they now were trapped in circumstance. More or less, they were slaves to men like Angus Monty. But when it came to Porter, Rabbit wasn't sure whether the man sailed with the philosophy of indentured servitude, but he was willing to give the barkeep a chance to prove himself.

He motioned Porter over and pointed at the food. "Help yourself, man, but fair warning—be nice to these girls, always. Help them. Protect them. Trust me, you don't want to get on my bad side."

Porter held his gaze for a long moment and then nodded.

A sharp whistle from over by the door flagged Rabbit's attention. Clementine sat with her elbows on the table while watching him. Her lack of smile and narrowed gaze made him wary. She beckoned him with a single finger.

What did she want now? Did she figure on telling him he wasn't just ignorant, but ugly as a buck-toothed buzzard, too?

He wanted to ignore her, but his curiosity won the game of tug-of-war. Fine. He returned his empty cup to the table, snatched up another, and headed toward her table. Then he stopped and returned to grab another cup of mead for her.

Sitting down across from her, he pushed one of the cups her way. "Merry Christmas Eve, Miss Clementine."

A fire smoldered in his belly. He couldn't be sure if it was the mead he had just gulped or his earlier anger still keeping the coals red-hot in there. No, not anger. Disappointment. Sadness.

She sipped from the cup. Her eyes went wide and then she nodded. "That's good mead."

"From Alexey and Dmitry."

"Ahhh, of course. It's from Hildegard's stock."

Rabbit stared at her as he took another drink from his mug.

The girls at the piano started in on a round of "One Horse Open Sleigh," but their version was entirely inappropriate for youngsters.

Clementine wrapped the cup of mead in both hands and eyed him over the top of it. "When I came of age and it was time to strike out into the world on my own, I had every intention of leading a solitary existence. It is the way my grandparents raised me, and there was solid reasoning behind their actions. I am a Slayer. Ideally, a Slayer's existence is singular. Barren. Forsaken almost."

She took another sip of mead, a small smile forming on her lips. "This is some of the best I've had, I think. It brings out the flavor more if you can warm it a bit."

He wrapped his hands around his cup, too, and waited. The faraway look in her gaze when it met his made it clear she wasn't done with the past yet.

"Since I knew nothing else but that solitary life, I accepted it. Most interactions with people were uncomfortable and often ended in harsh words or confrontations. I came to welcome my solitude in a way, although there were a few who I let inside my barriers." A shadow of pain darkened her face. "But in the end, my grandparents were right. Relationships, either fleeting or extended, were uncomfortable binds to be avoided at all costs. They left nothing more than painful memories to be eradicated in their wake."

Rabbit thought about trying to remove the people from his memories. Uncle Mort. Boone. All of his companions and acquaintances over the years, including the women who'd warmed his bed. But there was no way that would work. These people gave his past context. His memories were meaningless without those who helped make them.

He looked up to see her watching him with raised brows. "You can't imagine it, can you?" she asked.

He shook his head.

"Some people have a way about them." She paused for a drink. "And these people are dangerous, but not as adversaries. They are dangerous because they expose a weakness in me that can be exploited by the wrong sort." She stared toward the piano, her eyes narrowing as she sat up a little straighter. Her forehead tightened. " 'You must not let weakness compromise your duties, *Liebling*,' " she said in a deep, gruff voice. " 'You are a Slayer. All else must be abandoned.' "

Rabbit swirled the mead in his cup. "Was that your grandpa talkin'?"

She nodded, her features softening again. "You. Hank. Boone. You are all dangerous for me. Allowing you three to help me goes against everything my grandparents taught me." She grimaced. "If something happened to any of you, I don't know what I'd …" She cleared her throat and shifted in her chair. "It can't happen. Not again."

Rabbit began to understand. It wasn't callousness or disregard that drove her to push him and the others away. It was concern. Friendship.

"So, there were others?" he asked. "A man, maybe?"

She nodded once but explained no further.

It all made sense. She'd experienced loss before. Now, she was trying to stop the three of them from strong-arming their way into her life, and falling down like a cow on ice.

That reminded him of one winter day when Boone had needed to lasso a heifer who'd managed to land herself in the middle of a frozen watering hole and couldn't …

"Looky here! In my pocket!" Squeaky's voice cut through the laughs and singing and plinking going on at the piano.

"Mine, too!" Pearl cried.

"And mine!" Fancy squealed.

They all began to titter and chatter more loudly than before.

Goldurn it! Rabbit had hoped none of them would realize before he left the saloon that he'd given each some extra consideration inside the pockets of their flannels. It wasn't much, just a useful contribution to their well-being in the form of paper money.

The girls rushed Rabbit, surrounding him and Clementine. After thanking him profusely with hugs and coating his cheeks with kisses, a wave of "*Clementine!*" filled the room. The girls then doted on his *amiga* for a few moments, overflowing with smiles and giggles as they caught up with Clementine, who'd done her fair share of protecting the doves from abusive assholes who enjoyed giving bruises as well as pokes—or worse.

After several wishes of "Happy Christmas," the swarm dissipated as quickly as it had formed, leaving Rabbit alone with Clementine again.

His fading grin ran into her narrowed gaze and pinched lips.

Rabbit pointed at her. "I think I know that look."

"All of them, Jack?"

His eyebrows knitted. "Uncle Mort was a fine man. He did his best to raise me to be one. He taught me there are things a gentleman does and there are things a gentleman doesn't. One of them things he doesn't do is gallivant around talkin' about his *enthrallments*. That's what he always called them. He'd say, 'That more than likely will tarnish the reputation of the parties involved and sullies the character of the yammer-mouth what said it.' That's the long and short of it, according to Uncle Mort."

Clementine smirked. "Right."

Rabbit didn't sit comfortable with that smirk. "Now if a man *was* inclined to talk about such things, he might say he hasn't had enthrallments with," he swept his hand through the air, "*anyone* in this room."

One of her eyebrows lifted. "Anyone?"

"Anyone," he reiterated. "Although, being such a stellar gentleman, he wouldn't yammer on about such things."

Clementine tipped her head slightly, doubt still lingering in her gaze. "They are handsome women in spite of their somewhat lack of health at the moment. Even a so-called stellar gentleman would notice that."

Her disapproval stung like raw alcohol in a cut, but if he were honest with himself, Rabbit knew it was the reputation he'd fostered. Still, she needed to understand something about him if they were going to keep being good *amigos*. He rested his forearms on the table and hit her with a hard stare. "Maisy, the little one there by the piano, she's probably fourteen. She doesn't know for sure. Make you wonder why that is? You should."

Her cheeks darkened as his meaning hit her. "I'm sorry, Jack. It was wrong of me to presume. You are truly a stellar gentleman clear through."

He waved off her compliment, ready to change tack. "I need to go."

A quick survey of the room found Miss Mollie and her girls laughing and singing once again, munching on confections and roasted meat, gulping mead, hanging ribbons fashioned from bodice laces, and draping makeshift petticoat garlands from every nail head and post.

"Go where?" Clementine asked. "What of all this?"

"They'll be fine." He scraped his chair back and rose. "You can come along with me or not, it's up to you. If you want to get along to Slagton, I won't try to stop you."

He looked down into her gray eyes for a moment. The thought of her venturing out alone into the unknown dangers he knew awaited sat like an anchor in his belly, but he knew she had to make the choice to stay on her own.

He swallowed past a small lump of worry in his throat. "I'll see you around, Miss Clementine. Merry Christmas." With one last glance at Miss Mollie's girls, he headed for the door.

"Jack, wait!" Clementine joined him as he stepped outside. "Where are you going?"

"I need to make a visit to someone."

"I'll follow along, if you don't mind."

"That's up to you." Rabbit kept his voice level as best he could, but he was sure his face betrayed his delight at her sudden turn.

Did this mean she was delaying her trip to Slagton? Had something he'd said convinced her to stay? He pondered those notions as he navigated across and down the street a bit farther.

He glanced to Clementine as they walked. "Uncle Mort used

to say a thing I didn't ever understand. I think maybe I do now."

She leaned into a strong, face-freezing gust. "Your uncle must have been a hoot. Is he here now?" Clementine knew all about his uncle's ghostly visits.

"Not at the moment. Anyway, Uncle Mort used to say 'Adversity persecutes the forsaken.' Every time he said it, I asked him what it meant, but he wouldn't tell me. He'd just say, 'Remember me when you figure that out.' Ol' coot. Thought he was clever all the time."

"Adversity persecutes the …" Clementine frowned up the street. "You think you understand now?"

"Yeah, maybe. Because of you."

"Me?"

"Yep. You."

"Do tell."

Rabbit took a seat on the bench in front of the Grand Central Hotel, making room for her to join him.

After she sat down, he looked out at the street, watching the show in front of him. It seemed as if everyone was preparing for Christmas in some way or other. The peal of bells mixed with the sounds of laughter and singing, playing a far happier tune than the moans of sorrow and the shouts of anger and unhappiness that normally pervaded the street.

"Adversity persecutes the forsaken," he repeated and lightly elbowed her arm. "That's you."

"How am I adversity? I don't think of myself as adversity. Not so much as, well, maybe …"

"Miss Clementine," he interrupted. "You're not *the* adversity. You are livin' the adversity. What he was sayin' was, you are the forsaken. You gotta know how Uncle Mort talks to follow along with the old buzzard. *Forsaken* means different things for different people. I think that's what he meant, anyhow. For you, it means bein' alone. Solitary. You are a lone wolf, and you'll suffer the adversities of someone who has no one to help when help is needed."

Clementine was quiet for a moment. Then she sniffed and said in a stiff voice, "I've never *needed* help."

"Knowin' you, maybe not, but you could have used it, I'd wager. See, it never made sense to me what Uncle Mort said, because I always had Boone. He's been there lookin' out for me since we were little tykes. Always had my back." He paused, realizing that was a thing he'd taken for granted all these years.

Clementine went silent again, her face unreadable as she watched the cheerful hubbub up and down the street.

"I gotta go inside the hotel," Rabbit told her after a minute or two.

Without explanation, he left her there on the bench, heading into the hotel. He skirted the front desk and strode to the dining room. Taking one of the two open tables, he craned his neck, looking around for one particular serving girl.

The lacy curtains hanging in the windows each had a red bow tying them back to the wall hooks, and the white table linens were decorated with a single candle surrounded by several sprigs of pine. Otherwise, the hotel's dining room looked the same as always—crowded with too many tables, chairs, and people.

Before he'd located the young girl he'd come inside to find, Clementine scraped back the chair opposite him and settled into it. "What are we doing in here?"

"We are lookin' for someone." He saw the waitress then across the room. "There she is. Minerva! Over here!" Rabbit waved the girl to the table.

As Minerva approached and he got a good look at her, his heart ached. She appeared more wretched than ever, like a sheet of skin draped loosely over a skeleton, despite Rabbit's continued attempts over the last few weeks to bolster her both physically and mentally. He would be surprised if she was eating more than a watery bowl of soup now and then for sustenance. She must have been spending the coins he gave her on something other than food.

He glanced at Clementine, who was staring at Minerva with unmistakable dismay.

"Sit down, Minerva." Rabbit stood and pulled over an empty chair from the table next to them.

She smiled weakly, but stayed standing. "I surely would adore a respite, Mr. Fields, but I got too far back of my work already."

"Sit," he repeated more forcefully, pointing at the chair.

She sat down, but glanced repeatedly toward the kitchen door as if afraid it would swing open and a monster would emerge and gobble her up. "I can't lose this work, Mr. Fields. If the cook catches me on my hind end, I'm on the street for sure."

"You won't be on the street, Minerva." Rabbit pulled a brown paper envelope from the pocket inside his jacket and placed it on the table.

She looked down at it, scrunching up her face.

"Open it." Rabbit tapped on the envelope.

"Coffee! Where's that scrawny girl with my ham and potatoes!" A thick-necked, mush-headed brute on the other side of the room banged his fist on his table.

Minerva almost jumped out of her skin. She popped out of her chair.

"Sit back down." Rabbit gently tugged on her arm until she obliged. "Open that." He tapped the envelope again.

She touched it and looked at him. Was that hope in her eyes?

"It's a ticket for the stagecoach," he explained when she peeked inside the envelope. "You're going back to Charleston. Back to be with your family. No arguments this time."

"Mr. Fields." Minerva shook her head. "I told you. They won't receive me."

"They will. I sent a letter to your pa. Got his reply right

here." He pulled another envelope from inside his coat and dropped it on the table.

The mush-head banged his fist on the table again and stood with enough force to send his chair tumbling to the floor. "Get your scrawny ass in that kitchen and fetch my coffee and ham, wench." He started toward Minerva, but Rabbit shot out of his seat and headed him off. He saw from the corner of his eye that Clementine had his back.

"Miss Clementine," he said, glancing her way, "I'd surely appreciate if you would allow me the privilege of collaboratin' with the high binder comin' this way. He's about to be layin' right about where you're standin', and I'd just as soon you didn't get tangled with him on his way down to horizontal."

Clementine returned to her chair, but Rabbit could see by her posture that she was ready to strike like a coiled rattler.

He turned to face the mush-head, continuing to speak to Clementine. "You see, this rascal here has been no end of trouble to Minerva for a while now. We tried to teach him a manner or two without cracking bones, but I don't know. Maybe his skull is too thick and he can't get no idea through it."

The mush-head's nostrils flared. "I'm gonna snap you in half," he growled.

Rabbit measured the blunderbuss from head to toe, noting his clenched fists and forward lean. "Or maybe he's just plain dumb and stupid. Don't matter much which it is. Probl'y don't matter to Minerva either."

The mush-head took a swiping swing at Rabbit's head, but the brute seemed to be moving at half-speed. Without much effort Rabbit knocked the punch away with his right arm while delivering a thrusting jab up under the ribs with his left.

The brute let out a loud and breathy "*Oof,*" but then came around in a great arc with his left hand. He would have connected with the side of Rabbit's head but for that half-speed business.

Rabbit dropped down, letting the haymaker punch pass over his head, and then heaved his right fist up and smashed it into the underside of the brute's chin. He continued to push up with a burst of strength, lifting the brute to his toes and sending him toppling backward, where he crashed to the floor. His big body stilled, his eyes closing. Little white pieces of something lay on the floor around him.

Rabbit peered down. Tarnation! Those must be the mushhead's teeth.

A blur of movement rushed him from his left. He barely had enough time to snap out a kick. His boot found solid purchase in a set of ribs, the impact sending a jolt up his leg. The second attacker collapsed onto the floor, curled up while gasping for breath.

A commotion clattered behind him. He turned, his fists raised and ready for another round.

Clementine stood, scowling down at a motionless third scalawag. She brushed off her hands and looked over at him.

Rabbit grinned. "I had that one, too."

She grinned back. "Probably."

They both sat back down, eyeing the rest of the citizens in the dining room. Every last one of them suddenly became inordinately interested in items at their own tables, including a small stain on a linen tablecloth by one trembling patron.

Rabbit huffed once. "Now." He pushed the letter toward Minerva. "That's from your pa. He wants you back quick as you can get there. He always did. He says it was that mean-as-the-devil momma of yours who didn't want you back. I'm sorry to say it or maybe I'm not, but she died of consumption some months back. But your pa? He was hog-tied sideways to get my letter. Said he was fixin' to come look for you, just didn't know where to start."

Minerva stared down at the envelope, her lower lip quivering.

He pushed the two envelopes even closer to her. "You're goin' home, Minerva. Like I said. Letter. Ticket. There's enough money in there with the ticket to see you home."

A cry of happiness came from the scrawny girl. She stood and rushed over to him, hugging him around his neck.

"Okay then," he said, patting her on the forearm that had him in a near stranglehold. He raised an eyebrow at Clementine, who chuckled quietly and shook her head.

Minerva sobbed in his ear, her face pressed against his cheek as her tears dampened his neck. "Mr. Fields, you are the kindest-hearted specimen of a man I ever did meet." She snorted in his ear, continuing to sob.

"I don't know 'bout all that, but we're gonna get you home, Minerva, plain and simple."

She pulled back, nodding hard enough to practically make her teeth rattle, and snorted again before wiping her runny nose with the back of her hand.

"Minerva!" A deep voice hollered out from the kitchen. "They's dishes sittin' back here waitin' fer you, ya scrawny chicken legger!"

Rabbit was half-tempted to pay a visit to whoever was flapping his lips back in the kitchen, but then he eyed Clementine, who was shaking her head.

"Minerva," he said, focusing on the girl again instead. "You got anything of yours in this hovel?"

"No sir, I got nothin' nowhere."

Rabbit gently pushed her away and stood. "Shall we?" He offered his hand to Clementine, but she stood without any assistance. He took Minerva's cold, trembling hand in his and escorted her out the door.

Out in front of the hotel, he noticed Minerva shiver in the chilly afternoon breeze and slid off his sheepskin coat, wrapping it around her slender shoulders. "Head on down to the Liberty Hotel. I secured a room there for you. Your stagecoach leaves from out front of the hotel first thing tomorrow." He smiled down at her. "On Christmas mornin'."

"Mr. Fields—" she started, pulling tight the collar of his coat.

"The only words I want to hear from you are, 'I'm goin' home, Mr. Fields.'"

The pale-faced girl gazed at him, lower lip all aquiver again. "But ... but ... your coat."

"Whup!" He held up his hand. "What did I just say?"

Tears overflowed from her big brown eyes, streaming down her cheeks. "I'm goin' home, Mr. Fields." She gave him a watery smile and then turned away, heading toward the Liberty Hotel ... and freedom.

" 'Case you didn't understand, keep that coat to wear home!" Rabbit shouted after her.

She turned, smiling wide while waving, and then continued toward the hotel.

He watched her until he couldn't see her anymore, and then hugged himself, shivering in the freezing wind. "Too goldurn cold in Deadwood," he said to Clementine with a smirk. "Anybody ever say that before, you think?"

"This is nothing. You should visit the seaside where I grew up during a winter storm. You'd be frozen solid within an hour or two." Clementine stared off in the direction Minerva had gone, sniffing several times. Her eyes were a little shinier than usual. She dragged her gloved fist across her face, blowing out a breath while blinking fast a few times.

Rabbit looked after Minerva once more, searching for his sheepskin coat, but she was lost in the crowd. His shivering was spreading south to his legs. "This town would've killed that girl," he said under his breath.

"From the hand of a stranger." She squeezed his arm.

He glanced from her warm hand to her face, running into her steady gaze. "Huh?"

"Nothing." She frowned down the street. "I suppose we need to get back to the livery. You'll shiver your teeth loose without a coat."

"Not yet." He pointed in the other direction. "I got one more place to be. This'll only take a shake."

He didn't necessarily *need* to make this last visit, but he wanted to nonetheless.

"Where are we going now?"

He looked up the street in the opposite direction of the livery. It would take only minutes to get there, depending on the cooperation of the crowd, of course. Another cold blast almost set his teeth to clacking. "Miss Clementine, you don't need to come with me. I understand you better now. I get why you need to go to Slagton. The *alone* part still don't make much sense to me, but don't go changin' your priorities for me."

"I'm not." She shot him a quick grin. "It's turning out to be interesting following you around today."

"Okay, then we're gonna go ... no, wait. You'll see."

He led her down the street until they were standing in front of a building with a grand façade that outshone its neighbors like a bright star. The spotless yellow clapboard siding, white trim, and cornices were all strung with evergreen garlands, giant red bows, and great bunches of holly.

"Here?" She pointed at the ornately carved shingle with the words "The Dove" painted in a fancy script that was hanging over the boardwalk.

"Yep," he said, smiling up at the sign. His favorite place in town thanks to the fine bathhouse and the best cooks. Hildegard Zuckerman offered only top-rated services—whether it was hot baths or pretty faces. The Dove's madam also happened to be one of Clementine's confidants when it came to fighting sharp-toothed *others*, including those bearing the *caper-sus* mark.

A hard gust of cold air rocked him clear to his boots. *Sheeat!* It was cold as a winter day in Deadwood, as Hank liked to say.

Rabbit grabbed the door handle. Without a coat, he figured it was best not to tarry outside. "Here," he said to Clementine and pulled the door wide for her to enter first, following close on her heels.

Inside The Dove, Christmas had come in abundance. The white curtains that glowed pink from the many shades of red velvet furnishings were all tied back with gold-colored ribbon while tall candles flickered in front of the glass. More evergreen garlands and holly adorned the shelves, bookcases, and mantel in the main parlor, which was oddly empty for a change. Must be due to the holiday. Rabbit stood in awe for a moment, taking in the beautiful spectacle while his shivering stilled thanks to the crackling fire heating the room.

The hearty aromas of food baking and roasting in the kitchen had his stomach growling before he even realized he was hungry. Meats and breads and sweets were sure to be waiting on the other side of the kitchen door. The thought alone made his head spin. He inhaled deeper, picking up the whiffs of spices he hadn't smelled since he was in San Francisco—rosemary and ginger ... and cinnamon, too.

"I love cinnamon," he whispered in the quiet parlor, rubbing more warmth back into his arms.

"Me, too," Clementine agreed.

"*Fröhliche Weihnachten!*" Jurgen, the German doorman who specialized in taking out any riffraff who dared to cross Hildegard's threshold, stepped out from a side room and slapped Rabbit on the shoulder hard enough to make him stumble forward.

His shoulder stinging, Rabbit smiled at the block of solid muscle with a head attached. "*Frolicka wei* ... what was it now?" He figured it was some way or other to say "Merry Christmas" in German.

"*Fröhliche Weihnachten!* Merry is Christmas." Jurgen grinned at Clementine and then wrapped his bulging arms around her and picked her up in a vigorous German hug.

Clementine yelped in surprise and then laughed.

Jurgen was one of the few people that made Rabbit feel like a pony grazing among horses. Or more like draft animals. Better yet, oxen. The bruiser's arm muscles alone probably weighed more than Rabbit did even with his boots on and loaded down with guns, gear, and ammunition.

Rabbit took off his hat. "Well, then 'merry is Christmas' to you, too, Jurgen. Are the Russians in the kitchen? It sure smells like it."

"*Ja.*" Jurgen lowered Clementine back onto her feet. "You will say *Hallo* to them."

Rabbit wasn't sure if that was a command or a question.

"Is Madam Hildegard in?" Clementine crossed to the fire and rubbed her hands over it.

"No, *Fräulein* Clementine."

She frowned slightly. "If it's okay, Jurgen, I'll go to the kitchen with Mr. Fields. I'd like to see Dmitry and Alexey, too."

"*Ja.* You will go." He motioned them both to the kitchen.

Rabbit led the way. He swung open the kitchen door and walked right into an argument filled with deep voices and terse Russian words.

"*Da!*" Alexey noticed them first and hollered across the kitchen from his place at the flour-covered butcher block. Next to him, the massive, smoking cast-iron stove was doing a great job of heating the large kitchen, making it positively toasty. Rabbit could swear the stove was glowing orange-hot, doing double-time cooking every kind of dish from appetizers to meats to desserts, no doubt.

"Is good seasoning for duck when trussed and dressed like Mamochka's, but is not Mamochka's duck. Is Christmas duck. You forget much, but Alexey remember."

Dmitry, who was cutting dough into lines on the long plank table, pointed a large knife at his identical twin. "You remember that I am cook number one. You are cook number two."

"*Nyet.*" Alexey emphasized his rejection with a chop of the cleaver. His round face had drips of sweat running down his reddened skin.

"Mr. Rabbit! Clem! Welcome to kitchen!" Dmitry waved at them, his face splitting with a grin almost as wide as he was. "Happy Christmastime. Is good to be seeing. This is busy time for us but welcome. Cooking, cooking, all day cooking for Madam Hildegard. For Christmastime feast tomorrow. No. Is not correct to say. Correct to say, *I* cook." His grin shifted to his brother. "Alexey burn."

"You move lips but talking is not," Alexey said, setting down the cleaver and wiping his hands off on his well-used apron. "Is babbling like baby." Alexey took Clementine by the shoulders. "You look healthy. *Nyet*. How you say ... uh, good in looking."

"Is 'lovely,' *zhopa*. Word is *lovely*. Clem is looking lovely always." Dmitry grinned wide enough to show his top and bottom teeth.

Clementine chuckled, shaking her head as she looked at Rabbit.

Alexey moved to Rabbit, taking him by the shoulders as he had Clementine. "Greetings to you, Mr. Fields. Is looking strong and lovely, too, yes?" He looked to Dmitry for confirmation.

Rabbit laughed out loud. "Many thanks, boys."

There was an air about these two brothers. It was of jovial companionship, even though they argued endlessly, similar to the relationship he shared with Boone.

"Mr. Rabbit always is lovely and healthy." Dmitry came over and grabbed Rabbit's jaw in his stubby fat fingers. "Is needing shave. But not today, I think. Busy today. You come back after Christmastime. Dmitry will shave you, soft as butter."

"No, no, no." Alexey knocked Dmitry's hand away and took Rabbit by the jaw. "I shave. Dmitry uses old blade and does not see so good. He is old now."

Dmitry scoffed. "I am your twin. You are as old as me and I am as young as you."

"Listen …" Rabbit tried to break in.

"You are older five minutes," Alexey said, releasing Rabbit's jaw.

"Wiser five minutes he is meaning to say," Dmitry told Clementine.

At a distance Rabbit would struggle to determine who was who. Both of them were short, bald as babies' bottoms, and very round in the middle. But Rabbit wouldn't want to tangle with either one of them. As good as he was getting with his throwing and Bowie knives, from what he'd heard, these two could slice him into Rabbit meatballs and cook him in a sauce.

"We came here to talk to the two of you." Rabbit tried to interrupt their bickering again.

"Oh!" Alexey stuck his finger in the air. "We have *lebkuchen* fresh from oven. Chocolate. Madam Hildegard is fond for Christmastime. You will try. Dmitry?"

"*Da.* Here." Dmitry plucked two round, brown cookies from a tray sitting on the stove, giving one each to Rabbit and Clementine.

The cookie was warm, but not so much so that it prevented Rabbit from popping it whole into his mouth. A crunchy, chocolate sweetness coated his tongue. This was the best *lebkuchen* he'd ever had! It was also the first *lebkuchen* he'd ever had, but Rabbit was sure it would always be his favorite. He swallowed and looked toward the stove for another.

Dmitry appeared to have anticipated a need for a second one and handed another to him and Clementine, who'd polished off hers as well. Then the Russian began stacking the rest of the cookies on top of a piece of muslin. "I will wrap more. You will take."

Rabbit didn't argue. Neither did Clementine.

"Why are you here?" Alexey asked. "We are helping our two friends today?" He inspected them both with a narrowed gaze. "Mr. Fields travels without coat." He looked at Dmitry. "You will give him your old coat, *da*?"

"*Da*. I will fetch."

"No." Rabbit held out his hand to stop him. "I don't ..."

But Dmitry waddled-walked away, leaving through a door at the back of the kitchen.

"Miss Clementine," Rabbit whispered as Alexey opened the oven and slid in a roasting pan loaded with the carcass of a duck. "He doesn't need to give me his coat."

She shrugged. "You might as well accept it. Dmitry is a bit hard-headed."

More than a *bit*.

A moment later, Dmitry waddled-walked back into the kitchen carrying a heavy gray wool coat with white bone buttons. He shoved it toward Rabbit. "Is good coat. For you."

Rabbit took it, holding it up. A few dark stains crossed from one shoulder down the chest to the thigh flap on the other side. Was that blood?

"Thank you, Dmitry. It's a kindness." Rabbit smiled, patting the Russian's thick arm.

"Is good coat," Dmitry said again.

"Listen, I ..." He paused, glancing at Clementine, who was eyeing a fresh loaf of bread on the table. "*We* came to thank you both for the feast you sent to the girls at Yellow Strike Saloon. It was far more than I'd hoped for."

"Ah, yes." Alexey grinned at his brother. "Dmitry is good to the girls, yes?"

"Very good."

"Alexey is good too." Dmitry stopped stacking for a moment to glance at Rabbit. "They liked?"

"They were all titterin' like hens when we left. Oh. And that mead—"

"Is good, *da?*" Dmitry interrupted. "Very hard to bring to Deadwood for Madam Hildegard, but we do, eh Alexey?"

"*Da*. Is hard."

"Well, if you ever find a keg that needs a home," Rabbit said, pointing his thumbs at his chest. "I'll be obliged."

"Will see. Is difficult to bring to Deadwood." Alexey grinned at Dmitry. Dmitry winked back at whatever private joke they shared and handed Clementine the bundle of wrapped cookies.

Rabbit nodded, smiling. "Thanks again. You two are my favorite Russian cooks. Miss Clementine and I will take our leave, since you're busy."

As he and Clementine pushed open the kitchen door, Rabbit heard Alexey start in again with, "You hear? I am favorite."

"Alexey has bad ears," Dmitry growled. "Old? I am favorite. You put duck in too early."

Outside on the porch of The Dove, Rabbit slid into his new "old" coat. It fit better than he'd hoped. He stretched his arms out in front of him and the sleeves crept up his forearms, leaving his wrists exposed to the cold air. A tad short. He pointed at the stains slashing down across the front. "You think this is … ?" He trailed off as a pair of ladies strolled past them, biting his tongue.

"I'm almost certain," Clementine told him.

She offered him the muslin-wrapped *lebkuchen*, but he waved her off. Taking her by the elbow, he led her down the boardwalk a few steps.

"Miss Clementine, I wonder if you are willin' to make just one more quick stop with me?"

She didn't think long about it. "Why not?"

Good. If she was to go and risk getting herself killed in Slagton, then he wanted a certain piece of business finished before she left. "A little stop at the livery, then I'm done wastin' your time."

After walking next to him in silence for several steps, she

smiled at him. "You haven't wasted my time today, Jack. On the contrary."

That smile warmed him almost as much as the Russian twins' kitchen stove. He spent the walk back to the livery gabbing about his boyhood Christmases in Virginia, what he could remember, anyway.

When they arrived back at their starting point, she frowned at the closed main livery doors. "I'd rather not go inside right now."

Her reluctance was no surprise to Rabbit. If Boone or the Beamans were in there, it would be more difficult for her to go ahead with her plans to leave.

"Sure. I'll be right back." He shot through the side door in the livery and grabbed the present he'd spent hours fashioning for her. While part of him fretted that she would find it pointless or badly designed or a hundred other things wrong with it, he'd made up his mind to give it to her anyway.

Upon his return he simply said, "Merry Christmas, Miss Clementine," and handed her the linen-wrapped gift. "The bow isn't like what Hank could tie, but it'll do."

Her smile warmed her whole face. "It's very sweet of you, Jack." She took it and pulled at the twine bow. It didn't budge.

"Sorry. Let me get that." *Dingdang twine.* He slipped one of his throwing knives from its sheath and cut the twine.

She unfolded the linen to reveal a scabbard fashioned from the finest leather he could find. Her eyes widened. "Oh, my. This is beautiful!"

With Boone's help, Rabbit had determined which Norse symbols to carve into its length and enlisted their new blacksmith to help fashion the brass chape and locket. Beaman was a master with metal, there was no doubt, and Rabbit himself wasn't half bad with a beveller and a piece of leather.

"It's for the *Ulfberht*," he told her, referring to her favorite blade, which had been passed down through her family for generations. "You strap it on your back and then you can draw the blade up over your right shoulder, quick as a rattler. See there? That's the Norse symbol for good health." He pointed at the mark. "That one there is for ..." He paused trying to remember exactly what it was for. "For success in combat. Courage in combat here." He paused, realizing he, a native Virginian, was teaching a Norse woman about Norse symbology. "Well, you know better'n me."

She tenderly ran her fingers over the scabbard as if it were made of delicate lace. "It's the most beautiful leatherwork I've ever seen, Jack."

"I did it for you, Miss Clementine." He looked at the ground, toeing aside a lump of snow. "I didn't know if you wanted a scabbard for *Ulfberht* or something ..." Darn it, his tongue was starting to feel like it was trying to tie into a knot. "I just wanted you to feel like you got *amigos*, you know. It don't sound like you ever had *amigos* to watch out for you. You do now, is all I'm sayin'. If you want 'em." He scowled at the snow and decided he should shut his fat mouth.

After several seconds of silence, he looked up at her without raising his head. Was she mad? Was she laughing at him?

He caught the sight of a tear starting down her cheek before she brushed it away. Sniffing, she looked at the scabbard for a moment longer and then wrapped her arms around him. She squeezed him so tight he thought he would pop.

"Thank you, Jack," she whispered in his ear, kissed his cheek, and then walked away up the street.

With a crooked grin, Rabbit watched her disappear into the throngs of carolers and shoppers and merrymakers. Was he going to see her again? "Goldurn stubborn Northwoman."

After one last look, he headed into the livery.

Boone waited for him just inside the door. "Well? Did she like it?"

Rabbit shrugged. "Could be. I don't know."

"You think she still plans on going to Slagton by herself?"

"Don't know that either."

Boone scoffed. "You don't know much is what I know."

"Shut up, Boone. You're next. Let's see if you hold any sway."

"Right." He stared out the open livery door, his face lined up and down. "Wish me luck."

"Good luck. She's a tough nut." Rabbit squeezed his shoulder. "You got the book?"

"Right inside here." Boone patted the front of his coat over his chest.

"Bein' clear," Rabbit said as he walked his *compadre* out the door into the late afternoon sunshine. "She's not goin' to Slagton alone, right?"

Boone's dark eyes locked onto his. "Of course not."

STAVE FOUR

The Last of the Friends

*B*oone hustled and stomped through the slushy, muddy runoff of Deadwood's main street. The gentle incline of the terrain was good for removing melted snow and rain—and other, smellier manmade things, but it also allowed the runoff to carve irregular ditches and gullies through the street that created something of an adversity out of navigating the main thoroughfare, if one could call it that.

To make the matter of navigation worse, a few of the industrious sort had taken to first picking, then panning, and then digging trenches in the dirt and muck of the street, hoping the riches that were said to pave Deadwood were somewhere below, hidden by a layer of grime and …

Hmm, what is that? Boone skirted what looked to be a heap of … never mind.

He turned his attention to The Pyre funeral parlor a short ways up the street. Clementine was most likely in there, and it was his intention to challenge her.

She won't listen, said the cynical voice in his head.

She would, too.

Maybe. But you aren't going to change her mind. She's a loner. Nothing you can do to change that.

"Says you," he muttered under his breath.

Don't delude yourself.

"Clap the yapper, naysayer."

Fine! But you'll see.

He would see.

Maybe he was wrong to go to The Pyre to try to stop her. After all, Clementine was a clever, capable woman with clear sentiments about her place in the world. She was a Slayer; there was no ambiguity on that point. *And* there was nothing about that fact that he wanted to change.

Boone detected conflict in her, though. She had known only aloneness and seclusion for most of her life, but with the appearance of Hank came the possibility of friendship. He offered a platonic companionship; one that would appeal to anyone who desired camaraderie yet dreaded the encumbrances of a more emotional connection.

Then came the Sidewinders from Santa Fe. Both Rabbit and Boone had grown fond of her and, he believed, she of them. Clementine had helped them not only uncover the truth about Uncle Morton, but also dole out a reckoning to the *Bahkauv*. They hadn't necessarily avenged their uncle, but they were off to a good start.

Now Rabbit and he were in it, maybe not as deeply as Clementine, or Hank for that matter, but they were in it just the same. Add to that their ownership of the livery and the new hotel they were building, and they were now committed to life in the Black Hills, like it or not.

A blast of freezing air hit him broadside, nearly taking his breath away. Hurrying through the cold, Boone cursed Rabbit under his breath. It was Rabbit who had convinced him to stay in Deadwood—mostly. If it hadn't been for that headstrong mutton-puncher, Boone probably would have returned to the sunny warmth of Santa Fe. Winters there were a hell of a lot milder, and their uncle's ranch house was warm and comfortable, and often smelling like sweet pastries this time of year thanks to Lupe's love of baking.

Truth be told, though, that would've been a decision he'd have regretted for the rest of his life.

For one thing, he liked Clementine. Really liked her.

His thoughts got mired about why he *really* liked her for a few steps before he pushed them aside and returned to the track he'd been traveling along.

He also considered Hank a very good friend now. If he and Rabbit had skedaddled and left the two of them to face the corruption spreading in the Black Hills, he would never have forgiven himself.

Even though Clementine still insisted on going it alone.

He stopped under the awning of The Pyre with its rough-cut clapboard siding and shuttered windows, deciding on the spot that he was doing the right thing. Clementine was getting his help even if he had to hog-tie her to make her accept it.

His rap on the door went unanswered. His stomach sank with dread.

She left for Slagton already. The cynical voice was back.

"Calm down," he said under his breath. "She'll play hell trying to get Fenrir past Rabbit."

Boone tried the handle. It was unlocked. He pushed inside, closing out the cold behind him.

The parlor room was warm thanks to the fire crackling in the stove. The two cushioned leather chairs on each side of it looked soft and inviting. Clementine's parlor desk had been tidied up since the last time he'd visited, her chair tucked into it and the inkwell capped. He could smell a hint of jasmine in the room even though the incense stick on her desk wasn't burning.

"Clementine!" he called, wiping his boots on the entry rug.

"I'm in the examination room, Boone," Clementine hollered back.

He blew out a breath of relief and headed across the hall, stopping just over the threshold. "I hoped I'd find you here."

Clementine stood at her desk with her back to him. Her apothecary case was open wide next to her. His gaze traveled south along her thick braid, pausing on the curve of her hips outlined by her trousers before sliding down to her boot heels. Her aversion to petticoats and bustles was truly his fortune.

Boone stepped farther into the room, skirting the two wooden examination tables where Clementine plied her duties as an undertaker. There were no dead bodies sharing the room with her tonight, much to his relief.

The only other furnishings besides the tables and her desk were a small wood stove and a wall of cupboards—the contents of which were still a mystery to him.

"Well, not in *here*, exactly," he said, wincing slightly as he passed the tray of shiny, sharp tools she used when examining her horizontally inclined customers.

"I'm almost done," she said without looking his way.

He closed the distance between them.

Dark glass bottles littered the desktop in front of her. She dripped yellow liquid from a clear bottle into a flask, corked the bottle, and set it down. Then she gently swirled the flask for a few seconds. She passed the flask under her nose and smiled. "Perfect." She poured the liquid into a brown tonic bottle that she corked and set on the desktop before turning to him. "So, did Jack or Hank send you looking for me?"

He didn't answer that. Instead, he stared into her eyes, searching for some signal that she wasn't going to run off to Slagton yet this evening—or for something inviting him to go with her if she did. But she held her cards close to her vest.

He glanced down at the bottle. "Have you taken to making magical tonics, Clementine?"

An acrid emanation from something on her desk whirled past him suddenly. He recoiled, covering his mouth and nose with the back of his hand.

She picked up one of the uncorked bottles and waved it under his nose. "Does this offend your proboscis?" she teased.

He grinned, bumping her hand away. "That is an abominable smell. What is it? Pickled rat intestines or some such?"

A smile teased the corners of her mouth. "Close. Did you say 'abominable'?"

He shrugged. "What?"

Her smile widened. "Nothing."

"What?" he pressed.

"Oh, nothing, really. It's just that Jack may be right."

It dawned on him that she was teasing him about his choice of words. He decided to play along. "Offensive. That better?" He stepped back, taking a stroll around her exam tables. "Or repugnant, as in one never knows what repugnant odor might assault one's olfactory senses upon entering The Pyre."

"That much is true," she agreed, watching him closely.

He checked the woodstove, finding it cold to the touch. "Or nauseating. Obnoxious? Despicable. Horrible." He paused, having temporarily run out of words.

"That'll probably do, Mr. Descriptive." She crossed her arms. "Jack is definitely right about your extensive vocabulary."

"Oh! Repellent."

"Okay."

He rounded the table and stopped in front of her, closer than before. Close enough to see the tiredness lining her eyes and mouth. Or was that worry? "Maybe just plain stinky."

She slapped him playfully on the shoulder, her hand lingering on his sleeve. "Did you come to insult my abode, Mr. McCreery, or are you just here to ... that's an interesting coat." She touched the collar and then pinched the material. "What's it made of?"

"It's a gum coat. Uncle Morton got hold of a stack of gum blankets from the Civil War and had Lupe make coats out of a few of them. Rabbit has one, too."

"I thought Lupe was your uncle's cook."

"Cook, housekeeper, seamstress, and whatever else was needed of her."

She scraped her fingernails on the material. "What's it made of?"

"Cotton on the inside." He pulled the collar wide and flipped it so she could see the inside. "And rubber on the outside. Keeps a body warm and dry on a rainy freight run. See, water runs down past the top of the boots." He lifted his leg slightly. "Keeps rain out of your boots and the shins dry. The hood's big enough to go over a hat. Keeps that dry, too." He pulled the hood over his head. Without his hat on, it flopped down over his face. "See?" He flipped it back.

"Very practical." She ran her fingers down the sleeve. "I haven't seen you wear it before, have I?"

"Nope. The freight wagon from Santa Fe arrived."

Carlos had done an expert job of packing it for the trail. Everything had arrived in fine shape excepting three bottles in a case of tequila. Boone was inclined to feel sore about that since it was the good stuff, but overall it was a fine freight run.

He had hoped that Rabbit would be otherwise occupied when it arrived, since there were some things packed away on that wagon he didn't want his *amigo* to see, but of course he'd been front and center, ready to help unload. It had taken a handful of trickery on Boone's part to get the load stowed with Rabbit unaware of a few of its contents.

Clementine stepped back, leaning against her desk. "A gum coat. Huh."

"Yep." Boone pointed at the bottle she had just finished filling. "What's that?"

She picked up the bottle and handed it to him. "Smell it."

"What? I don't think so."

"Take the cork out and smell it." Her eyes dared him.

"Okay." He brought the bottle under his nose, preparing to take a small whiff. But before he did, he squinted down at her. "What are you playing at, Clementine?"

She pointed at the bottle. "Trust me, Boone."

He did.

Hmm. Cinnamon, cloves, ginger, other things he couldn't put his finger on. He could definitely smell rum, though. The concoction invited—no, it *seduced* him to take a drink. "What is this? I can have a sip?" He sniffed it again, his mouth watering a little.

"Sure." Her brow tightened. "But just one small sip."

He tipped the bottle toward his mouth, but then paused. "What's in it? Really?"

"Tail from rat and squishy eye of mole." She cackled and wiggled her fingertips at him. "You will be transformed into a great hairy troll."

He snorted. "Stop it."

"What a lily-livered streak you have!" The sparkle in her eyes took the sting out of her words.

He sipped from the bottle. The liquid coated his mouth and throat. It was at once warm and cool, spicy and sweet. It tasted of rum, his favorite liquor, and a crisp, juicy apple along with buttery smooth caramel. The complex yet smooth blend of contrasting and complimentary flavors absolutely denied simple description.

Rather than waste time trying to come up with more words, he considered drinking more. Before he realized it, he'd tipped the bottle for another taste.

"Ah! One sip only," Clementine warned.

Her hand snaked out. Before he knew it, the bottle was taken from his hand. "It's good then?"

He watched her insert the cork, still craving another sip. "Yeah. What's it for?"

"That's not important." She put the bottle next to a small, lumpy-looking satchel laying on her desk that appeared to hold yet another bottle. "I wonder if you would walk with me down the street a ways. I have an errand I need to …" She froze all of a sudden.

He reached toward her. "What is it?"

"Don't talk." She grabbed his arm and dragged him out into the hallway, pointing toward the door at the end of the hall. "Go! Now!" she whispered. "Out the back door. As quietly and quickly as you can." She nudged him partway down the hall before returning to the parlor.

He hesitated, tempted to follow her back to the front room, but she might have good reason for him making a hasty exit. He started for the back door only to slow at the sound of the front door opening.

"I didn't expect to see you today," Clementine said.

He hadn't even heard anyone knock. From the clear and unwavering tone of her voice, she didn't sound afraid of her visitor. So why did she rush Boone away?

"I didn't anticipate the necessity of this visit," a man replied, his voice as deep and smooth as good whiskey.

Without a second thought, Boone darted into her private quarters instead of out the back door. He glanced around her bedroom, which was lit by a single candle next to her narrow bed. He'd been in here before, several times in fact. It was where she kept all of her weapons locked up tight in a wall-sized cabinet.

Over along the wall, her bed was neatly made with what looked like a chemise spread out on it. He tiptoed over and stared down at the undergarment. An embroidered dragon covered part of the front. Its tail started down at the hem, its body swirled around the bodice like smoke, and its mouth breathed fire at the neckline.

His mouth suddenly dry, he reached toward it, his fingers curious, his imagination running rampant. The silk material was so smooth, so soft.

"What can I do for you, Masterson?" Clementine's voice jerked Boone back to the moment.

Masterson? Masterson! So, he was here.

Boone stole over near the open door to listen.

He had long wanted to meet the man who held Clementine's reins. At least that was what Masterson seemed to think. For some reason, the fool seemed oblivious that she would take the head of anyone who tried to control her. Then again, the relationship between Masterson and Clementine was undoubtedly more complicated than Boone understood.

The steady clunk of boots on wood told him someone was pacing. He doubted it was Clementine, though. She wouldn't attack Masterson outright. No, she would've established a defensive position.

"I believe we ..." *clunk clunk* "... care of the matter developing there, did we not?" Masterson's voice had a sharp edge to it.

Boone grimaced. He had missed a key part of Masterson's question, dang it. He moved a little more into the doorway, careful to stay out of sight.

The clunking sound of boots continued. Clementine's visitor was the one pacing, for sure.

"Of course," she said. "You know exactly what my plan is."

"Then why have you not proceeded?" Masterson was easier to hear now. Moving closer, maybe?

Boone's muscles tightened at the menacing snarl that had replaced the suave tone in Masterson's voice. Anger surged through him. He took a deep, soothing breath. Clementine could handle herself. Besides, revealing his presence might actually endanger her.

He stepped back from the doorway, inadvertently bumping a tall stick that had been propped against the wall. It slipped sideways, scraping the whole way down, and landed with a rattling thunk on the rough plank floor.

Consarn it!

Out in the parlor, everything went silent, including the clunking of boots.

As quiet as an owl, Boone squatted, snatched the staff from the floor, and then stood up again. The staff was a solid piece of oak almost as tall as he was. The head on it looked like the knurled fist of an old man. Intricate symbols had been carved into the wood here and there along the length of the oak. He tested the weight in his hands and swung it out in front of him.

Light and strong.

Yes, it was adequate to drub a "Masterson" at close range.

Silence reigned yet in the parlor.

Boone gripped the staff tighter and waited, breath held.

The boots clunked again, louder. Masterson was coming down the hall toward the back of the building—and Boone.

"Masterson!" Clementine's voice came from the parlor. "Here!"

The clunking stopped.

Boone strained his ears, holding the staff up and back, ready to strike. What was that sound? Was Masterson sniffing?

"Masterson!" Clementine repeated, her voice closer now. "We will attend to our dealings in the parlor. Now!"

After a long held breath, Boone heard their footfalls retreating. When he was sure they had returned to the front, he lowered the staff. His heartbeat slowed, steady once again.

"Your proclivity to harbor pets is unsettling," Masterson said. "Their odor displeases me. I must pause to consider my reaction." *Clunk clunk clunk.* "Shall I do away with the offending chattel? Or is this a time to display benevolence?"

Boone growled under his breath. *I'm a pet, am I? Chattel?* He could use a stiff drink to quench the fire that was working its way up his throat. Then again, that might make it burn even hotter.

"I don't have time for your musings, Masterson. This is The Pyre—a place of business. I receive visitors from time to time and you have nothing to say about it." Clementine stood her ground, her voice strong. "I told you, our plans haven't changed. I'm leaving for Slagton soon, so you need not fret."

The clunking of boots continued. "I don't fret." Boone could hear the contempt in Masterson's reply, loud and clear. "You've allowed the problem in Slagton to languish to an extent that I may need to involve myself. I am disappointed in the extreme with your performance."

Clunk, clunk, clunk. "You must go there immediately."

"I have errands to complete first. I will go when I am ready."

"If I had known that you would act the petulant child when I commissioned you, I would have chosen another. One who is more obedient. And competent."

Boone couldn't believe his ears. Didn't Masterson understand who Clementine was? What she could do with her blades when provoked?

"Stop the petty insults," Clementine said evenly.

"Remember your place, Slayer. Complete the tasks I've given you, or I'll relegate you to mucking stalls at the local livery for your friends. Or perhaps I should do away with the lot of you and start again!"

A resounding *crack* rang out, followed instantly by a *BOOM* that seemed to shake the building. Boone nearly dropped the staff. At the sound of the front door banging shut, Boone shook off his surprise and darted down the hall and into the parlor.

Clementine stood gazing out the window with her jaw clamped shut. She slowly shook her head.

"What happened? What was that? It's like the building was falling down."

Clementine frowned over at him. "Oh, that? It was just Masterson playing his games. He tries to be impressive with his displays. Sort of like a peacock. Comes up short, though, I think."

"He's a real horse's ass."

"That's an insult to horses." She turned her back to the window and took several steps toward him. "I told you to leave, Boone."

"Didn't quite make it."

He didn't admit that he could have but hadn't wanted to—and he wouldn't next time either, if it meant leaving her in jeopardy. After eavesdropping on her conversation, Boone was beginning to understand how dangerous an adversary Masterson was to her.

"Do you think I could take Masterson?" He jokingly swung the staff, nearly connecting with her shoulder.

She shook her head. "Don't even try."

He wasn't sure if she was protecting him, or if Masterson would kick his tail all the way back to Santa Fe.

"And stop swinging that." Clementine caught the staff mid-swing, holding onto it as her gaze narrowed. "Boone McCreery, you were in my room, weren't you?"

"Maybe." He thought about mentioning the pretty chemise to see if he could make Clementine blush, but then changed his mind. Uncle Morton had taught him better.

She let go of the staff. "On second thought, I've seen you fight. You might be able to give Masterson trouble." She raised an eyebrow. "What do you think of the staff?"

His face warmed a little at her compliment.

Or maybe it was the intensity in her gaze that made him flush.

Or thoughts he shouldn't be having about her chemise.

He made a point of focusing on the staff. "It's beautifully crafted. I imagine the symbols all mean something. Stout, but still easy to swing." He raised it again.

"It's not really meant to be a weapon, although it certainly *could* be used that way." She held out her hand for it and he passed it to her. She hefted the staff a few times and tapped it on the floor. *Thunk thunk.* "It's a Pathfinder staff. I had it made for Hank. The symbol on the top is a Norse compass." She admired it for a moment. "Beautiful work." She handed it back to him.

Boone took it and stared at the compass carving. "Hank will love it. It's thoughtful of you." He smiled at her. "And appropriate."

Just as that dragon on the chemise was appropriate for her, given her fighting skills. Where had she gotten that undergarment, anyway? From someone in Chinatown?

She jerked suddenly, as if someone had pinched her. "We should go! I've a stop to make. You'll accompany me?"

"Certainly." He wasn't likely to turn down a chance to spend time with her, especially since it gave him time to think up ways to keep her in town longer. He pulled his coat hood over his hat and headed for the door, staff in hand.

"Wait!" Clementine held up her finger and then disappeared into the examination room. She returned carrying the small satchel in which she'd placed the brown bottle full of her aromatic concoction. She slid into her wool coat, wrapped a thick red scarf around her neck, and donned her fur trapper hat. "Let's go."

Boone noticed two things upon stepping outside of The Pyre. First, the sky had gone gray, partly because of the setting sun but also because of a sheet of ruffled dark clouds that were sliding over the blue sky like a blanket pulled up over a bed. Second, energy Boone didn't normally experience in Deadwood emanated from the groups of people gathered in the street. The air was filled with cheerful voices. Laughing and singing rang out here and there. *Singing!*

In spite of Deadwood bustling with jollity, Boone still noticed the ordinary. A bout of fisticuffs was underway outside the Crusty Goblin Saloon, surrounded by a cluster of shouting men, which was no surprise considering the watered-down whiskey the owner of that particular establishment tried to slip past his customers.

As Clementine and he made their way down the street past the livery, he saw a man fly out of the front doors of the Belle Grande Theatre. Before he could get to his feet, the big brute manning the door picked him up and growled, "And don't come back, you lousy sot!" Then the brute kicked him, sending the man stumbling down the steps. At the bottom, he landed face first in the muddy slush of the street.

Boone pointed at the man with the staff. "Poor soul."

He hustled over and helped the gentleman to his feet, brushing at his mud-caked coat. The smell of whiskey was strong up close to the man.

"You're up. Okay, are ya?" Boone asked, wondering what transgression would warrant a foot to the rump and unceremonious dump in the mud on Christmas Eve.

Sobbing, the man nodded and then staggered into the crowded street.

Clementine joined him. "Your good deed for the day is done. Let's go." She started down the street in long strides.

Boone trotted up alongside of her before slowing a little to match her gait. "Your legs are too long," he told her.

Truth be told, he'd never met a woman whose head came above his Adam's apple until Clementine. An inch or two on her boot heels and they'd stand eye to eye.

"My legs are exactly as long as they need to be." She glanced his way. "You know you can't save everyone, Boone."

He spun the staff in circles at his side now that the crowd had dispersed a little. "Maybe I can't save everyone, but I'll help a man out of the mud."

She eyed him for a moment longer before focusing on the staff. "Why did you bring Hank's present along?"

He held it up, taking another look at the carving on the head. "What's this symbol again?" He poked the staff in front of her face.

"It's a *vegvísir*. A Norse compass." She pushed the staff down and away. "It points the way. Whoever bears that symbol will never get lost."

"A symbol does all that?" Boone didn't hide his skepticism. It was his habit to need to see the proof of a thing before he fell in line with it. That included Rabbit's fixation on finding so-called magical elixirs.

"You may not believe it, Mr. Misgiving," Clementine said, "but that is one of a set of runes that help describe the world around us. They were used by my people, but they were not actually created by humans like other verbal languages."

"So where did they come from?" He twirled the tip of the staff out in front of him. It was oddly amusing to wield.

She watched the staff for a moment. "Some believe Odin learned of them from *Yggdrasil*, the tree of life."

He nodded. "Right."

She huffed at his doubt. "Anyway …"

They trudged on, through slush and snow and periodic small crowds of sometimes drunk and often merry revelers.

The clouds won the battle in the sky, completely obscuring the setting sun and leaving an ambient gray and misty veil on the buildings and people in spite of the lanterns and candlelight spilling from the windows. But farther down the street the glow of lights began to turn red and blue and yellow and green—Chinatown.

As they drew nearer, Boone held the staff across Clementine's midriff to stop her. He stood, slack-jawed, admiring the hundreds of paper lanterns hanging from poles and façades and shingles and ropes strung across the street. More lanterns had been placed along the boardwalks and in windows and doorways. Tapestries hung against clapboard siding and fluttered in the cold gusts from store shingles like colorful curtains.

Boone hadn't seen such beautiful colors since … Well, not since Santa Fe and the Christmas celebrations he'd taken part in down there.

He lowered the staff, keeping his eyes on the colorful scene before him. "In Santa Fe, during the few days before Christmas, everyone would make bags or bowls from colored paper and cut or fold Christmas scenes or designs into them. Then they'd put candles in them and line the streets, or string them overhead like that." Using the staff, he pointed at the hanging lanterns. "The light would shine through the paper. It was so beautiful. We would gather in the street and drink warm *ponche*, which is a sweet juice made from fresh and dried fruits. Then we'd sing Christmas songs." He chuckled at the memory. "Rabbit's *ponche* was always a little spicier than anyone else's, if you get my meaning."

Clementine grinned. "I get your meaning." She shot him a look of doubt. "You sing?"

"Sometimes. My *ponche* tended toward the spicy side, too, thanks to Rabbit. Enough of that juice and just about anyone will sing, I imagine."

Clementine started out again. After a glance at the sky, she quickened her pace.

He followed her. "Still got it in your mind to head to Slagton today?"

Boone didn't want to hear her answer, but he had to do something. He knew that Rabbit and Hank were at the livery, packing up the saddlebags, haversacks, and horses, as Hank and he had planned while Rabbit kept Clementine busy earlier. They might be ready by now, but Boone couldn't be sure. He needed to give them more time.

"Yes," she said, sliding on her gloves without revealing any emotion. No fear or trepidation, either.

"Right." He dodged a pair of boys who were running down the street, splashing slush and mud along the way. "You know, I heard what Masterson said."

She stopped again and looked up at him. "So?"

"He talks of your friends being chattel or animals."

She nodded.

"Do you realize he treats you the same way?"

She didn't respond, only stared at him.

"You're nothing but an agent," he continued. "A minion to him."

Her chin lifted. "That's enough, Boone."

"Is that what you aspire to be? A tool? A weapon? A means to an end to be tossed aside as soon as you are used up, or unneeded? Or killed? Make no mistake. You are nothing more than that to Masterson. What I heard? I'd wager he doesn't care one whit whether you live or die. He said it right there in your parlor—he'll just get another Slayer. And another. What does it matter to him? You are expendable."

Her brow knitted into a deep frown. "You think you're telling me something I don't know?"

"Maybe. Maybe not. But I'll tell you this. I'd make a wager you haven't come across anything in your travels that prepared you for this." He spun the staff in a circle over his head.

She looked skyward. "What? Gray skies?"

"Funny. No. The things that are going on here. Tell me you've faced anything like the *Bahkauv* queen before." He waited.

She lowered her gaze to the ground.

"What would've happened if you'd faced her by yourself?"

She didn't answer.

"And the *Bahkauv* infesting these hills?" He didn't wait for her to speak. "If you're honest, you know there are too many." He waited for that to sink in and then continued. "And now we have who knows how many *Draug* out there. Not to mention *Höhlendrache* and skin eaters." Boone tugged at his collar. He was getting worked up, and whenever that happened, he got hot.

"I can handle it," she countered with a straight face. "I always have."

Jumped-up Jessie on a hopped-up Holstein! *Like talking to Fred the Mule, but I think Fred listens better.*

"I've told you before, Clementine, you're not alone anymore."

Rather than deal with her bullheadedness any longer, he pointed the staff down the street. "Let's get to where we're going." He started to walk away from her, letting the staff lead the way, but then paused and turned back. Frustration burned in his chest, stoked by a strong-headed, auburn-haired Northwoman. "You ever stop to think that maybe Hank and

Rabbit and I are here for a reason? Your Norse runes ever consider destiny or fate?"

Before she could reply, he headed down the street again without a single idea of where he was going.

She caught up with him shortly but didn't speak until she caught his arm and pulled him into an alley. "This way."

Still grasping his sleeve, she led him around the backside of several buildings toward a log-walled shelter covered with ragged canvas.

A knock on the pine-pole door brought a woman who looked decidedly more haggard than hale. Her countenance portrayed curiosity, but still, she held a tired smile for them.

"Greetings, Mrs. ..." Clementine paused with a small frown. "I know your name is Eunice, but I'm afraid I don't know your last name. I'm Clementine. I visited you earlier in the company of Hank Varney."

"I remember. Please come in."

Clementine ducked through the door and Boone followed, full of curiosity, but he remained silent.

"This is Boone McCreery." Clementine shot him a quick smile. "He is a friend of Hank's as well. He owns The Sidewinder ... oh, uh, what used to be Keller's livery toward the other end of town."

"How do you do, Eunice?" Boone pulled the coat hood off his head and tipped his hat toward the woman. "Pleased to make your acquaintance."

His focus returned to Clementine. Why in the blazes were they here?

"I came to see about Davey." Clementine fished the bottle of tonic from her satchel and held it out toward Eunice.

Davey? Who was Davey? Boone searched the room. There was an elongated lump in one of the two beds, covered with layers of blankets. The lump rose and fell in short, rapid breaths.

Ahh. That must be Davey.

Eunice looked at the bottle, a frown clouding her face. "Oh, Miss Clementine. Thank you, but …" She slowly shook her head.

"Please," Clementine said in a low voice and took a step closer to the doubtful woman. "I believe this will help him. The tonic from Doc Wahl won't do any good, and by all standards, it will probably make him worse."

Eunice continued to shake her head at the bottle. "Hank knows you, and that bears some weight. But I don't." She focused on Clementine, her eyes narrowing slightly. "You're that lady undertaker, aren't you?"

Clementine's expression hardened. "Yes."

"An undertaker knows more about medicine than a doctor?"

"I do. At least more than Doc Wahl." Clementine frowned over Eunice's shoulder toward the boy.

"Down in these parts, people say things about you." Eunice chewed on her lower lip, still measuring Clementine by sight alone. "They ain't nice."

Clementine huffed. "I don't really care what people say, Eunice. I just want to help your son. He has congestion in his lungs." She jiggled the bottle of tonic. "This will help him. Without it, he will most definitely …" She stopped short, but Boone knew where she'd been heading.

A rattle-filled string of coughs issued forth from the bed. The boy gasped for breath and then coughed again.

Eunice rushed over to check on the child, adjusting the covers before returning. "Listen, I trust Hank, but I don't really know you. I got to think of my boy. Doc Wahl knows what he's doing."

Clementine's jaw clenched. "Doc Wahl gave you a bottle of laudanum and whiskey," she bit out.

Boone put a hand on her shoulder. Her muscles were rigid. If Eunice wasn't careful, Clementine might just bind and gag the poor woman and administer the tonic herself.

"Eunice," Boone said, deciding to try to talk sense into the woman. "Miss Johanssen knows medicine. She makes tonics for most things that ail a body. She even saved my dog Tink when death came knocking. I promise you, she wouldn't do anything to hurt Davey."

Eunice eyed his companion. "You say the undertaker here knows medicine, but I hardly know her." She jutted her chin at Boone. "And I don't know you at all, Mr. McCreery. Now, the two of you might have the best intentions, but I don't know that from a chicken on Sunday."

A chicken on Sunday? What the ...? "Eunice—" he started.

"Naw, no." Eunice shook her head quick and hard. "I got to trust Doc Wahl." She moved toward the door. "You two best leave now, before Lester comes home. He finds you here, no telling what might proceed."

"Eunice!" Clementine started after the woman, reaching for her. "What kind of mother—"

"Okay, Eunice." Boone snagged Clementine by the coat and held her in place. "We'll be on our way. But maybe Clementine can leave the tonic and tell you how much to give him."

Clementine's eyes were rimmed with anger. Boone held her stare and raised an eyebrow. "Well?"

After a loud sigh, Clementine said, "One spoonful, every three hours. You shouldn't need more than what's in that bottle, but if you do, come to The Pyre." She set the bottle on the table and then pointed at it. "That will save your boy's life, Eunice."

Boone tugged on her arm. "We'll be going now, right, Clementine?" When she didn't answer or budge, he tugged harder and kept tugging all the way out of the dilapidated cabin and back down the alley to the street.

Clementine yanked her arm away from his grip, glaring down the alley. "She'll kill that boy with her ignorance."

"It's her boy. You've done your part. Now it's up to her to follow it through. That's not your task. It's hers."

She raised her hands in the air and growled at the sky.

Boone shared her frustration, but he also accepted that the boy's life was in his mother's hands.

"He'll die," she ground out.

"He may. He may not."

"He will!"

"She may give him your tonic and it doesn't help." Boone reckoned the tonic would probably work, but a little doubt might take some of the sting away.

She pursed her lips at him. "Not likely." After one last look down the alley, she bolted up the street toward The Pyre, a full head of steam propelling her.

"Whoa there, steam train!" Boone trotted up next to her. After matching her stride, he asked, "Where to now?"

"I have work to do."

He was relatively certain that meant Slagton.

"Stubborn as Fred the Mule is what you are," he grumbled.

"That, Mr. McCreery, is a compliment."

As they wound their way through the scattered revelers inhabiting the street, Boone caught a glimpse down an alley of four or five men, not much more than boys by the look of them, bent over a pile of rags or clothing. Adolescents, probably. He stopped to consider the scene.

Not rags.

It was a man.

Boone started toward them.

The man on the ground wasn't moving.

He quickened his step. "Hey now!"

One of the boys was yanking the boots from the man's feet.

Boone began to trot. "You there!"

Two more were pulling the coat from the man's back.

Yet another appeared to be searching the man's pockets while a fifth stood by and watched.

"STOP!" Boone pointed the staff at the muggers as he ran

into the alley.

His raised voice caught their attention. Two ran immediately, disappearing down into the misty darkness of the late afternoon. Another finished tearing the second boot from the man's foot and followed the first two. The last two stood, and faced him, each brandishing long thick blades. Neither boy said a word, just watched him, their faces gaunt and wary.

Boone roared, "Odin owns you!" He repeated the words he'd heard Clementine yell in the heat of battle and raised the staff, readying for a great swooping swing.

The two boys glanced at each other, and then stared back at Boone, their eyes wide.

Boone released a battle cry, "Ahhhhh!" He charged at them.

They turned and shot in the opposite direction, bumping and tangling in each other's feet and arms. One nearly went down before they disappeared around the corner and into the misty labyrinth of buildings and tents.

Catch those urchins! Boone huffed after them.

"Boone!" Clementine's voice stopped him. "Don't follow them into that maze."

He took a deep breath, his ire subsiding. She was right, of course. Any or all of those young men could be hiding around any corner, waiting to ambush him with knives or clubs or worse.

Boone trotted back to Clementine, who was squatting beside the motionless victim.

"Is he alive?" he asked, kneeling next to her.

"Just. He won't regain consciousness." She pushed to her feet and placed her hands on her hips, frowning down at the man. "It's probably best. His hands and arms and feet are frozen almost solid. There's nothing I can do to help him."

"There must be something." Boone had to try. "We can't just leave him here. We should take him to The Pyre. It's likely he'll end up there one way or the other, anyway. Might as well offer him some dignity in death."

Clementine shrugged and then nodded. She lifted the man's arms and helped Boone maneuver him over his shoulder, carrying Hank's staff as they left the alley. The poor soul was so small and emaciated that Boone had no trouble carrying him the short walk it took to return to The Pyre.

By the time Boone laid him out on the examination table, the man was dead. Clementine set aside the staff and donned her work apron, spending several minutes checking the body for signs of *caper-sus* and whatever else she did, about which Boone was perfectly happy to remain ignorant.

As she worked, Boone stared out the window. It was dark now, except that it wasn't. In spite of the biting gusts whistling through the gulch, a parade had moved slowly and steadily up the street. Along with it came a contingent of Chinese, carrying more paper lanterns. The multi-colored light swirled and swayed with each step of the lantern carriers; the glow danced across the buildings and snow, to and fro. The misty fog that had moved in and blanketed the town added a colorful glimmer that seemed to emanate from the air itself. It mesmerized him, reminding him of the splay of colors from the prism he used to hold up to the sun in his room when he was a boy.

"So." Clementine's voice dragged him back to the present.

He turned away from the window.

"There are definitely no signs of *caper-sus* on the body." She moved over to the candle on her desk and scribbled in the notebook Boone had seen her use before to document information on the bodies passing through The Pyre. "Almost definitely death from exposure."

He wasn't surprised. Boone didn't know how many lost their lives each week in Deadwood due to the cold, but he figured it was a lot.

Clementine quickly finished her examination and wrapped the body in muslin. Then she pulled a little wooden boat from her desk drawer and tucked it into the wraps of fabric near the center of the man's chest.

At his raised brows, she explained, "That will help carry him to the afterlife."

Boone smiled at her thoughtfulness.

"Let's take him out to the shed." She lifted the dead man's feet and waited for Boone.

A short time later, with the body neatly stored in the shed behind The Pyre to wait for the gravediggers, Ling and Gart, Clementine started coffee on the stove in the parlor.

It was evening by the time they were sitting in the pair of leather chairs enjoying the warmth of the fire, eating *lebkuchen* cookies, and listening to the wind gusts rattle the roof. Every now and then when old man winter would pause to catch his breath, Boone could hear the faint sounds of the piano from a nearby saloon, along with waves of drunken laughter and singing.

"It's sad," Clementine said. "I wonder if he had a family." She sipped at her coffee.

"Probably. Maybe not." Boone looked over at her. She still wore her trousers and boots, but she'd changed her shirt after working on the dead man. Tendrils of her auburn hair were slipping free from her braid, curling around her face. "He's you. You know that, right?"

Her knitted brow told him she didn't know that. "What do you mean?"

"Tell me about him."

"His features were of a normally statured but undernourished man in his mid- to late thirties."

"His clothes?" Boone prodded.

"They were tattered. Worn out. The clothes that weren't stolen, that is. I would imagine the items stolen were in the same condition."

"His hands?"

She shook her head, her brow still knitted. "Why …"

Boone raised an eyebrow.

"His hands were those of a man who—"

"Those of a man who hasn't worked with his hands until recently," Boone finished. "They weren't hardened and calloused as you would expect from a miner's hands or a farmer's hands."

"What's your point?"

"See, a body adapts to the conditions it's subjected to. Look here." Boone held his fingers up for Clementine to inspect. "See the calluses between my fingers? That's from holding sets of reins. The reins on freight teams. You don't normally see that on a man who swings a pickaxe, or on a farmer, whose hands are covered with one big callus."

"Okay, okay. I understand." She looked up from his hands. "But what do you mean he is *me*?"

"I'll explain it to you, but first I'll tell you that man's story." Boone took a long sip from his coffee to wet his throat. "He came to Deadwood to make a success of himself. He probably already was a success of some sort somewhere, but it wasn't enough for him. He wanted more. More money. More power. More recognition. I don't know what else, but he wanted it, and figured here was the place to get it. Only he didn't find that. He found hardship and scarcity."

Clementine watched him with her head tipped slightly.

"For whatever reason, he was stranded here, unable to return to his previous life. He had to find a job. To eat. To pay for a two-bit room shared with twenty other men in need of a bath and shave." He paused to take another sip of coffee.

Her brow furrowed. "How could you know that?"

"His hands. Only brutal work tears up the hands like that. Now if he were accustomed to it, they would be calloused and hard. No, like I said, probably all put together not a full day's work swinging an axe or hammer. They were like a child's hands. Soft. But then torn up by hard labor."

"What does this have to do with—"

"Indulge me for a moment." Boone leaned forward and rested his elbows on his knees, holding his palms close to the stove to warm them. "He took the job, but had already lost his strength, or he wasn't fit for the task, so they used him until he had nothing left to give, then tossed him aside. Worthless." His gaze centered on hers. "Sound familiar?"

"That's ridiculous. That doesn't describe me at all."

"It does. It's precisely what Masterson is doing to you."

She shook her head.

"I'll tell you what else I see."

"Why not? I probably couldn't stop you anyway." She was tense now with stiff shoulders, sitting up straight.

Boone laughed. "Nope. I expect not." He rose and topped up their cups with steamy, hot coffee. "You're like the urchins robbing that mostly dead man."

"I am not."

"You are, if you allow yourself to be self-critical for a spell. You accept your task from your master and then you slay. When you're finished, you pick over your prey and abscond with anything you deem worthy." He pointed toward the hallway leading to her room. "Your cabinet back there is full of weapons you've scavenged from your conquests. Tell me I'm wrong."

"I don't know if 'scavenged' is an appropriate characterization of my ... rewards. Besides, you're wrong. It's only partly full of those weapons. The rest were mine to begin with."

Chuckling, he sank back into the leather chair. "Right."

She scowled at him over the rim of her coffee cup. "Boone, did I ever tell you that you talk a lot?"

He loosed a full belly laugh.

As the night wore on, they talked more of Masterson and *others* and Rabbit and Hank. And then of Christmas, both in Santa Fe and those from Clementine's past.

"I sure wish you'd let us look out for you," he said, setting his empty cup on the floor. "Go with you to Slagton."

She studied her hands that were clasped in her lap. "If anything happened to any of you," she started, and then frowned, shaking her head.

"Well, at least spend Christmas with us tomorrow at the livery." *Christmas* ... "Oh! Desert daisies! I almost forgot." Hopping up from his chair, he began rummaging through his gum coat hanging on the coat tree. He pulled the brown paper–wrapped gift from the inside pocket and handed it to Clementine. "This came in that wagonload from Santa Fe."

"Oh." She turned the package over and then back upright. "Is it a gift?"

"Sure. For Christmas."

Her eyes softened. "Boone, you don't need to—"

"Just open it." He returned to the chair and the warmth of the stove.

She tore at the paper, pulling out the book he'd wanted her to have. She looked up at him, her gaze searching for meaning.

Boone smiled. "It's *A Christmas Carol* by Dickens."

"I see." She set it in her lap and ran her fingers over the well-worn cover. "Thank you. I don't have many books. They're too hard to travel with."

He leaned forward in the chair, reaching out to touch the cover as well. Memories flickered through his mind. "It's the same book Uncle Morton read to us on the days before Christmas every year. We'd all sit by the fire and he would read one stave each night for the four nights leading up to Christmas, and then read the fifth and final on Christmas Day. He did voices for the characters and everything." Boone's throat tightened. This would be the first Christmas his uncle wouldn't be around to ...

Clementine caught his hand in hers, stopping the sad notions building in his head. He looked up to find her watching him, her eyes glistening in the candlelight.

His heart pounded in his ears at what he thought he saw in her gaze. "I'd be happy to read some to you," he whispered.

She smiled, squeezing his hand. "I'd like that, Boone. I'd like it a lot."

He was more than happy to do whatever it took to keep her looking at him that way.

She handed over the book and settled into the chair, stifling a yawn as he flipped open the cover.

He didn't even make it to the second stave before Clementine slumped over in her chair, fast asleep.

"Tomorrow then," he said softly and closed the book, setting it on her parlor desk.

After stoking the fire as quietly as he could, he covered her with two blankets, carefully tucking them around her to keep the cold away. Then he plucked the key to the front door from her desk drawer and stood over her for a moment.

She looked so peaceful and lovely in the candlelight, not a glimpse of a deadly Slayer to be found.

He smiled. It seemed Slagton might wait until Christmas Day after all.

He blew out the candle and leaned close to her. "Good night and Merry Christmas, Clementine Johanssen," he murmured and brushed a feather-light kiss over her forehead.

After one last look at her snuggled up in the chair, he slipped out the door and locked it behind him.

STAVE FIVE

The End of It

Clementine spun in a circle, swinging her sword at arm's length. She was gasping for breath with sweat covering her, soaking her clothes. Cold. Exhausted. Afraid. Alone. Waves of ... what were they? She could see her foes in the growing darkness and was sure that she knew them, yet she didn't know. She couldn't describe them, but knew what they were. There were scales and horns and claws. Their fetid stench made her gag.

She looked up at the darkening sky. Her heart pounded as shadows rushed toward her. She was surrounded, suffocating with terror. Her movements now slowed by unseen resistance. She was losing the battle. She could feel it in her gut.

In the distance, the silhouette of an enormous horned creature roared and spread great wings. The thundering cacophony that followed made her cringe. She leaned against the ominousness of it, struggling to stand but crushed by the heavy dread that weighed down upon her.

Then, suddenly, she was ringed by three luminous figures. Squinting against the nearly blinding brightness, she watched as they rushed toward the dark beasts, forcing them ...

Tap tap.

She looked around her, searching the thickening shadows. Strange. What was ...

Tap tap tap.

She forced open her heavy eyelids and then jerked upright.

Where am I?

She blinked the sleep away along with her nightmare. Quickly, it began to return to her.

Boone.

The book.

She was in The Pyre.

Tap tap tap tap tap.

Bright, unveiled rays of the early morning sunshine spilled in through the window. She looked down at the blankets tightly wrapped around her and then held her hand out toward the stove. It radiated no heat.

"Merry Christmas, Miss Johanssen," an unfamiliar, gravelly voice greeted her, coming from within the parlor.

But nobody was there with her.

She looked toward her exam room, thinking maybe her visitor waited for her in there. Through the open doorway she could see dust floating languidly in the rays of light shining through the windows. She listened, barely breathing, waiting for the rustle of clothing or scuff of a shoe.

Silence.

Huh. Maybe her mind was playing tricks on her.

Out of the corner of her eye she saw something move. She glanced back and did a double-take. In the chair opposite her, or rather just above the chair, sat a man watching her.

She shot to her feet, the blankets falling to the floor.

He was older with gray hair and beard. His face was pale, almost colorless, but yet it seemed to shimmer and ripple as she stared at him. He wore a long nightgown of pale blue that seemed to undulate around him as he sat smiling at her. A nightcap rested a bit crookedly on his head, making him appear more comical than threatening.

"Do you understand now?" he asked her, crossing one leg over the other. A pair of worn boots dangled in mid-air, one foot bouncing as if to a happy tune.

She took a step toward him, a notion clicking into place. "Morton?" she whispered, wondering if he was the remnants of her dream.

"At your service." He bowed his head slightly and the nightcap shifted forward a little. He chuckled and adjusted the cap back to its original crooked position. "Makes me happy as a bee in butter I won't be consigned to only talking to Jack from here on out. That boy sure can make a labor out of a conversation." He rose to a standing position, his feet floating just above the floor, making him as tall as her. He shifted closer, sizing her up with one squinty eye. Then he leaned back and grinned wide. "You do understand now, Miss Johanssen."

Understand what? "Call me Clementine," she whispered. "Or just Clem."

"Clementine. You're right. That's better."

Tap tap tap tap tap!

The rapping at the door snapped Clementine's attention away from the ghostly figure standing before her.

"You have a guest," Morton said, drifting toward her desk. "I'll be going. But I will see you at the livery later, yes? Those boys of mine need a wrangler, lords with buckets if they don't."

He paused near the book Boone had given her, staring down at it. A glimmer of melancholy passed over his features. Then he shook his head a little and when he looked back over at her, his grin had returned.

"But first," he continued and held up his index finger. "A Christmas morning constitutional about town, I should think. It is, by all standards, a glorious morning. A merry Christmas to you, my dear Clementine."

Morton bowed at her, and then he glide-walked over to the door. He reached for the knob but his hand passed through. "Dangnabbit!" He glanced back at her with a wrinkled brow. "Not acclimated to that still, it appears."

She chuckled. "Nor I to you, Morton. I have a feeling it shall be a merry Christmas indeed, and an even more interesting New Year now that I'll be able to watch you tease Jack."

He let out a full-bodied belly laugh and melted into the door, disappearing, leaving a faint iridescence on the wood in his wake.

Tap tap tap tap tap tap tap tap tap …

Oh, right! Someone was at her door.

Clementine hurried over and swung it open.

There Eunice stood, her fist still raised mid-knock. At the sight of Clementine, her expression shifted from a worried frown to a mixture of awe and apprehension. "I was afraid you might not be in, Miss Clementine. I was just preparing to leave but had to try one last—"

"Merry Christmas, Eunice." Smiling, Clementine held the door open for the woman to step inside.

"A happy Christmas to you, Miss Clementine." Eunice joined her in the parlor. A faint smile set upon her face after Clementine closed the door.

After a quick study of the haggard woman in the light from the window, Clementine couldn't tell for sure if Eunice was there with good news or bad. Davey's mother looked much the same as the last two times—weary and ashen.

"What is it, Eunice? Did you give Davey the tonic?"

Considering the way she'd left things with Eunice the evening before, it was doubtful. Yet still, she held some small amount of hope for the boy.

"I certainly did, Miss Clementine." She took Clementine's hand in her cold grip. "My trust in Hank. Your saintly demeanor." Her smile grew on her gaunt face. "It took me but the twitch of a cat's whiskers to trust you, too."

Tears filled Eunice's tired eyes and began to stream down her face.

Clementine watched the woman's tears with a knot in her throat. Was the boy gone? If Eunice administered the tonic, then he should be on the mend. But possibly she made a mistake in the delivery. Maybe she'd given him too much. Or not enough.

She squeezed Eunice's hand slightly. "How is he?"

"Oh, Miss Clementine. Little Davey is ..." She broke off with a sob, wiping at her tears.

Oh no! Please, great Odin, no!

"Little Davey is what?" Clementine pressed, her heart pounding.

Eunice sniffed. "Well, I gave him a spoonful every three hours, like you said, ever since last night shortly after you left."

"Good. And?"

A hiccupping snort came from the poor mother. "Davey sat up this morning. He sat up and spoke for the first time in almost four days." A fresh batch of tears filled Eunice's eyes. "He sat up and told me he was …" She sobbed once more, shaking her head. After another sniff and hard swallow, she whispered, "… hungry!"

A wave of warmth washed through Clementine, leaving her feeling rummy with happiness. "I'm gladdened to hear it." She walked over to her desk and pulled a handkerchief from one of the drawers.

"I thought I had lost him," Eunice said, pausing to blow her nose in the handkerchief. "But you, my angel, came to his rescue." She squealed suddenly and then wrapped her arms around Clementine, holding her tight, smashing her face into Clementine's shoulder. "I don't know how you did it, but you saved him," she wailed in a muffled voice.

As the weary woman continued to hug her, an impulse struck Clementine. She enfolded the petite mother and hugged her back, letting go of her loneliness, allowing her heart to rule her actions. She hugged her with such gusto that for a moment Eunice's feet even left the ground. The joy of Davey's turn back toward good health filled Clementine with warmth that no fire could match.

After they parted, she offered, "Would you like some coffee, Eunice?" Then she remembered that the stove was cold.

"No, thank you, Miss Clementine." Eunice blew her nose once more. "I must return home directly. It's almost time to give him another spoonful." She dabbed at her eyes and then held out the wilted handkerchief toward Clementine.

"You keep it. I have more."

Eunice stuffed it inside her coat. "I just wanted to thank you and to say that I would give you the world for saving my boy, but I have nothing."

"Nonsense." Clementine squeezed the woman's shoulder as they walked to the door. "You've given me the gift of trust. In my opinion, there is no greater."

Outside, the sun lit the street in a golden hue. The world seemed to be glowing. Clementine nestled deeper into her thick shawl. The air felt a tad warmer than it had in days. Or maybe it was just that the wind had finally stopped.

Eunice smiled up at her. "All at once, you are my dear friend. I hope you'll call on me if ever I can repay you."

"You already have." Clementine beamed along with the sun. She couldn't help herself. The joy she felt in saving a life rather than taking one was palpable. "Let me know how Davey is faring."

With a nod and a wave, Eunice left for home.

"Clementine Johanssen!" a man called from across the street.

She searched the sea of folks strolling the streets for the caller. In spite of the cold winter morning, laughter and shouts of joy filled the air. From the saloon down the street, she heard singing mixed with a plinking piano. The town was alive with Christmas cheer. And so was Clementine.

Across the way, a man waved at her.

She hesitated, trying to place his face. "Ahh ..." What was his name? She knew he was employed at the mercantile a few buildings up the street from The Pyre.

She returned his gesture, unsure why he would hail to her in the first place.

"A merry Christmas to you!" He called over the hats and fur-lined bonnets. "No castigations needed on this fine day, to be sure!" He waved again and continued on along the street.

Then she remembered. Months ago she had made a point of "castigating" a foul-mouthed, ill-tempered denizen who couldn't seem to keep his hands off the younger female clientele in that mercantile. The man across the street was the clerk behind the counter that day, and the smile on his face at the time displayed his feelings on the matter.

"Miss Clementine!"

She turned to see Mollie Johnson jiggling up the boardwalk toward her, her bosom puffing out above the fur collar of her long green coat. A ribbon-wrapped bonnet sat high on her coil of curls with two white feathers poking straight up into the air.

"Hello, Miss Mollie." She was genuinely pleased to see the madam from Yellow Strike Saloon on such a fine morning.

"Happy mornin' to ya," Mollie said in her twangy Texas drawl. She reached out and grabbed Clementine's hands in her soft velvet gloves. "The girls and me wanted to thank you for the festivities yester eve. They're still drinking mead and whoopin' it up this morning."

"You're welcome, Miss Mollie, but that wasn't me. That was put on by Jack Fields."

Her painted lips curved in a secret sort of smile. "He is a wonderment, no doubt."

Clementine wouldn't argue that point. Although, she had a feeling her reasons for singing Jack's praise were based on sentiments quite different from the madam's.

Mollie reached into her pocket and pulled out a small linen-wrapped and lace-tied package. She handed it to Clementine. "This is for you. The girls and I wanted to let you know how much we appreciate your friendship throughout the year. Your kindness, thoughtfulness, everything. We just wanted to thank you." She held the package out.

Clementine took it, looking from the package to Mollie. "Shall I open it now?"

"If ya like," she replied with a smile that made the morning sun shine even brighter.

Clementine untied the ribbon and unfolded the linen cloth to reveal a shiny silver hair comb with a floral design that had pearl beads at the center of each flower. She gasped. "It's beautiful, Miss Mollie. Thank you."

"It was Ginny's. The only thing she owned, really. We thought you should have it. You were such a good friend to her."

Clementine's throat tightened as the memories of pretty young Ginny flooded in with her bright smile and big brown eyes. Her friendship with the young prostitute had been stronger than Clementine had realized. But then, she tended to discount things like that. Friendship. Companionship. Good will. Ginny had confided in her, and Clementine had accepted the confidence, not grasping the depth of it.

A lump grew in her throat. Poor Ginny. She'd been a delicate, beautiful flower that had been swallowed up by the ugliness that lurked in Deadwood. Clementine had remedied that particular ugliness, the one with the name of Finnigan, but it had been too late for Ginny.

"It's pretty, same as she was," Mollie said, staring sadly at the comb. She broke from her memories and looked up at Clementine, a smile returning to her face. "A merry Christmas to you, Miss Guardian Angel."

Clementine blinked away tears, shaking her head at Mollie. "I'm not an angel, trust me."

Mollie touched her arm. "Neither am I, honey. But we can't let that slow us down." She gave Clementine a saucy wink and then headed back down the boardwalk.

"A joyous day to you, Miss Mollie!" Clementine called after her. "And your wonderful girls!"

Back in the parlor, Clementine stood immobilized by a dilemma. Yesterday, she had intended on making the journey to Slagton to address the problem of *Draug*. Then, as Boone read from the book he'd given her, she'd fallen asleep. Odd. It was almost as if Boone had put something in her coffee.

No. He wouldn't do that.

She was sure he wouldn't.

She dropped back into the leather chair, stymied into inaction by a maelstrom of feelings. Her duty as a Slayer pulled mightily on her. It always had. *Slayer above all else*, her afi had said.

But now ...

Something had changed. While the notion to take care of business in Slagton still needled her, her need to visit the men at the livery overpowered all else. Hank. Jack. Boone. Her friends. A longing to spend time with them, to talk to them and laugh with them, to share food and drink and merriment with them pulled at her with a force she couldn't resist. Nor did she want to. Not anymore.

She sat still as a stone, pondering this feeling as the world celebrated right outside her door.

Suddenly, it came to her. Morton was right. She did understand now!

She leapt to her feet. A warm tickle started in her chest and flowed upward, erupting into laughter. She rushed down the hall to her bedroom. After changing into fresh clothes, including her new silk chemise, she gathered the gifts she'd meant to give the three of them prior to leaving for Slagton, but hadn't found the nerve. Nor the time.

Those scalawags had detained her for the entire day, but she couldn't possibly be angry with them. She shoved all her gifts but Hank's staff into a burlap sack, including the book Boone had given her. They were her friends. Her companions. Of course they would do everything they could to keep her safe, the same as she would them.

With the presents tucked away and Hank's staff in hand, Clementine shrugged on her coat and ventured out into the bright, sunny world. Her stride was long, and she worked to quicken it. She couldn't get to the livery fast enough.

She paused halfway to the livery to wish good tidings to John Beaman and his daughter, Amelia, who were destined for a Christmas breakfast with a companion John had known since working on the railroad. Then she was on her way again.

Her pace was so livened that she managed the distance in half the ordinary time, even with the wishes of "Merry Christmas" and "Joyous New Year" that were frequent—and unexpected—which she returned with no restraint. The ear-to-ear smile she wore lasted the entire walk.

A lightness of heart filled her, as if the weight of a great boulder had been lifted from her. It was the realization that she had companions now, she was sure—*amigos* who cared for her, and for whom she could care in return.

As she neared the front of the livery, she stopped to admire the enormous wreath hung above the door. It had been assembled from evergreen bows and pinecones and ribbon.

"Beautiful!" She smiled inside and out, and then she opened the livery door. "Merry Christmas, one and all!" she hollered, leaving Hank's gift outside the door for the moment.

Fenrir whinnied in return. Several more whinnies followed, along with a few snorts and one loud, distinct *whinny-haw* that echoed throughout the livery. She chuckled. That would be Fred the Mule.

Hank, Jack, and Boone rose from the chairs set around the makeshift table near the blacksmith forge at the back of the livery. As she approached, their faces showed a mixture of surprise and relief.

"Good morning, gentlemen!"

"Mornin', Miss Clem," Hank said, his voice solemn.

"Good morning, Miss Clementine." Jack tipped his hat.

Boone pulled his leather gloves on as he stared at her with a raised brow. "Ready, then?"

She lowered the burlap sack to the floor, noticing that Boone was wearing his travel gear. As were Hank and Jack, too.

All were bristling with weapons—guns, knives, swords. Their horses and Fred the Mule stood chomping on feed off to her left. They were saddled and geared with bedrolls, saddlebags, and haversacks, all prepared for a long ride, including a fray at the end of it.

Fenrir, however, remained in her stall, bareback. The black Morgan whinnied again, much louder, and then Clementine heard her hoof scrape the floor several times. Fenrir was raring to go, too, and clearly not happy about possibly being left behind.

"What's this?" Clementine turned back to the men, frowning at each in turn.

"You're not going to Slagton without us," Boone stated.

"No, ma'am," Hank joined. "You'll not be gallivantin' across the countryside on your lonesome."

Jack shook his head and then patted his holster. "Your *compadres* are ready to ride."

Compadres. Friends.

Tears welled up for the second time this morning, darn it. She giggled. "You crazy bunch of sweet, delightful, compassionate, courageous men. We're not going anywhere."

The three of them exchanged befuddled glances before turning back to gawk at her.

"What?" Boone was the first to voice his puzzlement.

"We're having Christmas right here." Clementine looked around, admiring the decorations she'd seen Amelia starting to put up the day before. "In this wonderfully decorated livery."

The big barn would be the perfect place to spend the holiday, thanks to the Beamans' hard work. The entire interior was aglow, thanks to the shiny tin ornaments hung throughout that were no doubt smithed by Mr. Beaman himself. Shaped like dogs and deer and fir trees, along with angels and horses, birds and fish, each ornament had been suspended with particular care to catch and reflect the sunlight streaming through the upper windows. One enormous star that was the width of Clementine's outstretched arms dangled over the blacksmith forge by a chain similar to what Amelia had been dragging around yesterday. Maybe it was that same chain. Clementine's gaze moved to the star. The light from an attached lantern glowed through the patterns cut into the star's surface. Bows of evergreen and pinecones lined the stalls, stretching toward the majestic Christmas tree covered in bows that stood near the table and forge.

Clementine sighed. It was the most enchanting thing she had ever seen.

A ruckus of white fur tumbled and loped down the stairs, shooting toward her, accompanied by staccato yips and yaps.

"Tink is comin' to say 'Merry Christmas.' Look out!" Jack tried to divert the dog but missed. Tinker slammed into Clementine's thighs, yipping and barking and dancing circles around her legs.

"Merry Christmas to you, too, Tinkerdoo." Clementine reached into her burlap sack and pulled out a sow's ear. "This is for you. Or Jack. I can't remember which now." She winked at Jack and held the ear out to the dog. Tinker yipped and snatched the ear from Clementine's hand, immediately dropping to her belly to gnaw at it.

Clementine rummaged through the sack. "Yours is in here somewhere, Jack."

"Hoo hoo!" Hank took off his hat and dropped it on his chair. "Miss Clem got you a sow's ear, Jack Rabbit. That'll make a supper for ya!" He clapped Jack on the back.

Clementine chuckled and pulled out the bottle of tonic she'd prepared the day before. "Merry Christmas, Jack." She held out the bottle, a ribbon tied around the neck, toward him.

He took it, a toothy grin plastered on his face. "For fun? Or healin'?"

She shrugged. "A bit of both."

"Is that the one you—" Boone started.

"Mixed yesterday." She finished for him. "Yep."

"Mind if I try a wash?" Boone reached for it.

Jack bobbled his head and held the bottle away. "Tonics and elixirs are for the weak-minded, somebody once said." He pointed at Boone.

"Fine." Boone crossed his arms. "But I guarantee, once you open that bottle, it's gone." He tried to peek in Clementine's sack. "What else you got in there?"

She smiled. "Let's see." She made a show of rummaging in the sack. "I don't think there's anything else in here." She stuck her head partly in and pulled it back out. "No. Nothing else."

Boone nodded knowingly. "I can see bulges in there, Clementine. You got me something."

"Oh, Hank! I almost forgot." Clementine looked back toward the livery door. "Your present is right outside the front door there."

"Miss Clem, you didn't have to do no such thing." Hank trotted toward the door, obviously pleased that she did do such a thing.

Clementine exchanged a look of anticipation with Boone as they waited for Hank to return.

"Well, I'll be a fritter fried in duck fat." Hank rejoined them, holding the Pathfinder staff.

"It's a purty piece of work, sure 'nough." Hank swooshed the staff through the air. "I'll wallop a beastie or two with this."

"Why is it you men think everything is a weapon?" She sent Boone a wink. "It's a Pathfinder staff, Hank. It'll help you find your way—our way—when the path is uncertain."

Hank smiled at her so big his whole head north of his beard crinkled, then he squeezed her tightly in a bear hug. "Thank you, Miss Clem."

She laughed, squeezing him back. It was the best hug she'd received in a long time.

"That's a *vegvísir* on the top," she explained after he let her free to breathe again. "Legend has it, anyone wearing or carrying that will never lose their way."

Hank looked at it reverently, nodding, and then he grinned. "Guess that makes me lead scout. You two fellers better fall in and listen to me from now on." He shook the staff at Jack and Boone. "Goes for you, too, little Tinkerdoo."

Tinker paused her assault on the sow's ear to look up at him, her head tilted. She let out a snappy bark and returned to the ear.

"Hoo hoo! Foolin' with ya is all."

Clementine reached into her sack and pulled out a muslin bag full of hard candies. "These are from Hildegard. We can share them." She tossed the bag to Hank.

Then she reached in and pulled the last gift from the sack, handing it to Boone. He stared at the folded piece of soft leather in his hands, his brows drawn together, apparently not quite sure what to do with it.

"It's a chamois made from the skin of a deer. I worked it myself, and sewed the Web of Wyrd symbol on the corner. There, you see?" She stepped closer, pointing down at her needlecraft, feeling a fair amount of pride at how well it turned out.

"Web of Wyrd," Boone repeated.

"It symbolizes the connection between the past, present, and future."

"Hmm." Boone studied it. He seemed lost in the symbol.

"Now you gone and did it." Jack nudged Clementine's shoulder. "He'll study that 'til I dump water on his head."

She chuckled and then returned her focus to Boone and the symbol on the chamois. "It's the connected destiny of everything," she explained, not sure if Boone was getting the significance. "The past affects the present, the present affects the future."

"Fate," he said quietly.

"Exactly. But on a more practical level, you can always use it to clean your rifle and pistol."

He studied it for another moment and then folded it carefully and slipped it into his vest pocket. The warmth in his gaze when he looked down into her eyes made her stomach flutter. She gulped. *Oh, boy.*

"Thank you, Clementine," he said in a low, velvety voice.

The livery door slammed open, making her jerk in surprise. She turned in time to see Dmitry step through, followed directly by Alexey. They grunted and struggled with a wooden barrel resting on a net of rope between them.

"*Schastlivyy prazdnik!*" they called out in unison and labored toward the table near the forge.

Two porters trailed the Russians, one carrying a crate and the other a platter.

Jack hustled to the table and patted the keg. "Dmitry, is this what I think it is?"

Brushing his hands on his apron, Dmitry replied, "It is what you are thinking it is, Mr. Jack Rabbit, if you are thinking it is mead."

Jack and Boone cheered and started looking for tin cups.

"Compliments of Miss Hildegard." Dmitry bowed.

"My friends. Cups are here." Alexey tore the top from the crate and pulled a stack of porcelain cups from within. He began filling them and setting them on the table.

"You will find cheeses," Dmitry said. "Mr. Jack Rabbit and Miss Clementine know. From yesterday at Yellow Strike, *da?*"

"Thank you, Alexey. You, too, Dmitry." She hugged each of the twins. "This is wonderful!" Clementine took a cup and sipped. It was just as delightful as the mead the day before.

Dmitry squeezed her shoulders gently. "Miss Hildegard would be happy for your presence at The Dove for song and dances this evening."

"Well?" Clementine looked to her companions.

Hank and Boone grinned and nodded.

Jack rubbed his hands together. "Now that's what I call a Christmas present!"

The Russians and porters departed quickly, no doubt returning to tasks that awaited them at The Dove, leaving the four of them to revel in the candies, meats, cheeses, and mead from Hildegard and her crew.

Clementine had almost filled her belly when she realized who they were missing. "Where are Ling and Gart?" She sipped some mead, considering how long to wait before filling her plate with food again.

"They'll be along," Hank said, layering cheese and sliced meat so high he could barely hold it. "You see my new LeMat, Miss Clem?" He stuffed the stack of food in his mouth and pulled the pistol hanging from his hip while he chewed. "Got a pistol barrel on top and a shotgun barrel under." Crumbs flew from Hank's mouth and his muffled speech was difficult to understand, but his eyes were lit with excitement. "Boone gave it to me. Holster for it is from Jack Rabbit. Fine leatherwork." Hank lifted his coat to display the wonderfully tooled leather.

"Where did you learn to work leather that well, Jack?" Clementine asked as she studied the patterns cut into the holster.

"That would be me," a gravelly voice said from behind her.

"Uncle Mort." Jack turned with a scowl. "She asked me, not you."

"Fine. You answer." Morton—or rather, Morton's ghost—began to twirl and sway to unheard music. The sight of him in his nightgown and nightcap as he danced made Clementine grin.

"Uncle Mort got me started," Jack said, not realizing she had heard his uncle speak, nor that she could see Morton spinning about in merriment.

Morton floated up next to Clementine. "As I said earlier." He gave her a wink and then floated away again, his belly laughs echoing through the livery.

"It's beautiful," she told Jack. "Hank, what did you give the Sidewinders for Christmas?"

"Let's see," he said, scratching his head. "Good tequila for Boonedog." He looked over at Jack with a big smile. "And a seafarer's book of knots for Jack Rabbit to help with his piratin'."

"He gave me a type of tequila I haven't seen before, but one of the best I've ever had." Boone raised his cup of mead to Hank. "I suspect he went to some trouble to get it."

Hank nodded back at him. "And happy to do it."

"What else did I miss? Jack, what did you give Boone?"

"A Mark Twain book—his latest. It's called *The Adventures of Tom Sawyer*. Now he'll probably never shut his yap about it." He socked Boone in the arm. "It's just a book, you ol' skinner."

"It was perfect, Rabbit. Thank you."

They looked at each other for a moment, exchanging a look that spoke of a deep, old friendship.

"I was just about to give Rabbit his present when you came in, Clementine." Boone rose and motioned Jack to follow.

They all followed Boone across the livery to the grooming stall where Boone pointed at a saddle on a stand.

Clementine leaned back against the wall, giving Jack space. It wasn't a remarkable saddle; the ornate leatherwork was worn completely away where a leg rubbed or a strap was cinched countless times. The horn was wrapped in leather strips, the original leather obviously worn through. It looked to be a piece with little use left and even less value.

"Is that …" Jack froze and then slumped. He turned to Boone, his eyes watery. "What did you do?"

"It had to come." Boone's eyes were suddenly red-rimmed, but he took a deep breath and regained his composure.

Jack didn't. A tear streamed down his face, then another. "With the freight from Santa Fe?" he whispered.

Boone nodded.

"Hey." Morton appeared beside Jack, looking down at the saddle. "What's my ol' saddle doing here?"

"I thought we decided it wouldn't fit," Jack said. "What did you do?"

Boone hesitated.

"Tell me," Jack insisted, swiping at the tears.

"I took my show saddle out and put Uncle Morton's in."

Morton floated over next to Clementine and whispered, "Boone loved that show saddle. He worked many a long winter night tooling the leather and fixing it up real fine. It was the finest piece of leather you'd ever see. Every surface had been tooled in the most ornate fashion. Rosettes and basketweave covered the whole of the seat jockey and skirt. Oak leaves alternated with turquoise buttons to line the cantle and run the length of the billet straps and edge of the fender. Every piece of metal from the rigging dees to the buckles sparkled and shined."

"Aw, Booney," Jack said quietly. "You didn't." A fresh round of tears washed down his face as he stroked the saddle lovingly. Then he turned and grabbed his *amigo* in a hug, burying his face in Boone's shoulder. A quiet sob escaped from Jack, his breath hitched.

Boone stood motionless with his eyes closed, holding his friend.

After a moment, Clementine heard Jack whisper, "Thank you, my brother."

Clementine looked away for a few seconds, blinking away tears.

Hank blew his nose loudly in his handkerchief, breaking up the heartwarming moment.

"For you, Rabbit." Boone patted Jack's back once more before stepping back. "Well ..." He cleared his throat. "We should get to reading Clementine's book if we're going to make it to Hildegard's in time for the dancing."

Jack dried his eyes on his shirtsleeve. He shook his head at Boone. "I knew you were trying to hide things when we was unloadin' that wagon, you shyster."

"Yeah, well, look who's so smart," Boone teased back. He turned to Clementine with a raised brow. "You brought the book? Or do I need to go get it?"

"I have it." She thumbed toward the chairs. "In my sack."

"You'll do voices, just like I did, right, Boone?" Morton asked as he floated alongside of them all the way back to the forge.

"Uncle Mort says you gotta do voices, Booney, just like he did." Jack pulled the rocking chair in between the Christmas tree and the forge. "Keep you warm while you read."

"This whole livery is warm from this here forge." Hank dropped two large chunks of coal on the forge fire and poked at the glowing embers.

They refilled their cups with mead and sat, Boone in the rocking chair, the rest of them on chairs scattered around the forge. He opened the book and started reading from the beginning.

Morton floated over to Clementine and leaned down near her ear. "So Boone gave you that old book I used to read to them, did he?" he whispered.

She nodded, glancing toward Jack to see if he noticed his uncle talking to her. But Jack was leaning back in his chair with his eyes closed, focusing on Boone's voice. Or the mead. Or both.

Clementine closed her eyes and took another sip of the sweet mead. Jack was on to something. Boone's voice was hypnotizing. He had a way of making the story come alive.

"Did he tell you how I come by it?" Morton asked quietly in her ear.

She shook her head, listening as Boone read about Scrooge and Marley.

"I got it from his momma."

Her eyelids flew open. Boone's mother?

Morton was smiling sadly toward Boone. "She told me once on the wagon trail that it was her favorite story. Said she planned to read it to Boone and his sister every Christmas Eve until they were all grown." He glanced back at Clementine, still wearing his sad smile. "When they all died, I made sure to pack that book on back to Santa Fe with us."

The lump was back in her throat.

Morton floated next to her in silence for a moment, listening to Boone read. Then he chuckled. "What we have here, Clementine, is a bit of a catawampus Christmas celebration. It's a good thing ya got me along to make it even merrier."

Then, without another word, Morton twirled away, singing and dancing toward where Tinker still sat chewing on her sow's ear. When the dog wouldn't give him the time of day, he floated off through the wall of the livery, same as he had Clementine's front door earlier.

Boone's mom's favorite book.

He'd brought it all of the way from Santa Fe to give to Clementine. Her heart thudded hard in her chest. *Boy, oh, boy.*

She turned back to the motley crew before her, smiling at each man in turn, ending at Boone. Who'd have known that she'd find such a treasure in Deadwood? Three loyal, wonderful, loving friends. For the first time in a long, long time, she wasn't alone in this world.

As for Dominic Masterson and his orders and threats?

Clementine smirked. *Bah humbug!*

The End ... for now

Book 4 in the Deadwood Undertaker Series will be coming your way in 2021!

Merry Christmas!

Ann + Sam

The Deadwood Undertaker Series

Deadwood (late 1876) … A rowdy and reckless undertaker's delight. What better place for a killer to blend in?

Enter undertaker Clementine Johanssen, tall and deadly with a hot temper and short fuse, hired to clean up Deadwood's dead … and the "other" problem. She's hell-bent on poking, sticking, or stabbing anyone that steps out of line.

But when a couple Santa Fe sidewinders ride into town searching for their missing uncle, they land neck deep in lethal gunplay, nasty cutthroats, and endless stinkin' snow. Their search leads them to throw in with Clementine to hunt for a common enemy.

What they find chills them all to the bone and sends them on an adventure they'll never forget.

More Books by Ann

Books in the Deadwood Mystery Series

- Nearly Departed in Deadwood
- Optical Illusions in Deadwood
- Dead Case in Deadwood
- Better Off Dead in Deadwood
- An Ax to Grind in Deadwood
- Meanwhile, Back in Deadwood
- A Wild Night in Deadwood
- Battling the Heat in Deadwood
- Don't Let It Snow in Deadwood
- Gone Haunting in Deadwood
- Deadwood Mystery
- Evil Days in Deadwood

Welcome to Deadwood—the Ann Charles version. The world I have created is a blend of present day and past, of fiction and non-fiction. What's real and what isn't is for you to determine as the series develops, the characters evolve, and I write the stories line by line. I will tell you one thing about the series—it's going to run on for quite a while, and Violet Parker will have to hang on and persevere through the crazy adventures I have planned for her. Poor, poor Violet. It's a good thing she has a lot of gumption to keep her going!

About the Authors

Ann Charles is a *USA Today* bestselling author who writes award-winning stories that are splashed with humor, mystery, romance, supernatural, and whatever else she feels like throwing into the mix. When she is not dabbling in fiction, arm-wrestling with her children, attempting to seduce her husband, or arguing with her sassy cats, she is daydreaming of lounging poolside at a fancy resort with a blended margarita in one hand and a great book in the other.Facebook (Personal Page):
http://www.facebook.com/ann.charles.author

Facebook (Author Page):
http://www.facebook.com/pages/Ann-Charles/37302789804?ref=share

Twitter (as Ann W. Charles):
http://twitter.com/AnnWCharles

Ann Charles Website:
http://www.anncharles.com

Sam Lucky likes to build things—from Jeep engines to Old West buildings to fun stories. When he is not writing, feeding his kids, attempting to seduce his wife, or attending the goldurn cats, he is planning food-based booksigning/road trips with his wife and working on one of his many home-improvement projects.

Sam Lucky's Website:
http://www.samlucky.com

Made in the USA
Coppell, TX
18 February 2021